THE WORLD'S BEST-LOVED

Fairy Tales

TREASURE PRESS

First published in Great Britain in 1986 by
Treasure Press
59 Grosvenor Street
London W1

Translated from the French by Angela Wilkes

Illustrations © Editions Lito-Paris
English Text © Octopus Books Limited 1985

ISBN 1 85051 126 8

Printed in Czechoslovakia
50627

CONTENTS

Charles Perrault's
CINDERELLA

Retold by Françoise Chapelon
English Translation by Angela Wilkes

Once upon a time there was a nobleman whose first wife died. A year later he married a widow who was snobbish, hard-hearted and very bad tempered. The widow had two daughters by her first marriage and they were just like her in every way. The nobleman also had a daughter, but she was gentle, kind and charming. The stepmother could not stand her husband's daughter, as the girl's sweet character only made her own daughters seem all the more dislikeable, so as soon as the wedding celebrations were over, she gave the girl all the nastiest household chores to do. She had to do the washing up and scrub the bedrooms of her stepmother and stepsisters from top to bottom.

While the stepsisters lounged around in elegant bedchambers with polished floors, the most fashionable beds and full-length mirrors, their poor sister slept on a lumpy straw mattress in the attic. She bore these humiliations patiently and did not dare complain to her father as he was completely under his wife's thumb.

When the girl had finished her work she would go and sit in the corner of the hearth among the cinders from the fire, so the others mockingly called her Cinderella.

Yet in spite of her old and dirty clothes, Cinderella was far more beautiful than her sisters in all their finery. Her rags could not hide her long, blonde, silky hair, nor her pretty oval face and huge, inquisitive blue eyes. She had a fair complexion and a tiny waist and she was always smiling in spite of all her misery. Cinderella radiated calm, goodness and kindness. Nature had not, however, been so kind to her sisters, whose faces were as ugly as their characters. They had sallow skin and small, spiteful eyes, long, hooked noses, mean mouths and big yellowish teeth which stuck out. Their chins were receding and their hair was so dull and thin that they had to cover it up with elaborate wigs.

No matter how much make-up they wore, the sisters could not

disguise their ugliness. But they never stopped trying, and spent many hours in front of the mirror.

Now the king's son was to give a ball and he was inviting all the most important people in the land to it. The two ugly sisters were invited because they came from a good family. They were absolutely delighted and immediately set about choosing what to wear.

'I will wear my red velvet dress and my gold jewellery,' announced the eldest sister.

'And I will wear the dress embroidered with gold thread and my diamond brooch,' said her sister.

The whole house was thrown into turmoil as the two sisters

rummaged through their wardrobes, looking for the petticoats, corsets and lace trimmings which went with their dresses. Poor Cinderella had to wash and iron everything for them. The sisters tried on their dresses time and time again, as the hems and frills had to be altered, then posed in front of their mirrors, fiddling with their make-up.

When they were finally satisfied, they called to Cinderella to come and do their hair, and she arranged it with the greatest care and skill. While she was kindly doing this, her sisters taunted her mockingly.

'How would you like to go to the ball, Cinderella?'

'You are just making fun of me,' replied Cinderella.

'You're quite right,' sneered the ugly sisters. 'How everyone would laugh if *you* went to the ball!'

Anyone other than Cinderella would deliberately have made a mess of the sisters' hair, to pay them back for their spite, but she was too good-natured and did the best she could.

Eventually the sisters were all dressed up and ready to go, and their coach set off for the palace. Poor Cinderella sat at the window and watched it disappear into the distance.

'How lucky they are to be invited to the ball by the king's son,' she sighed. 'How I'd love to go to a ball in a beautiful palace glittering with lights! It would be wonderful to meet charming ladies dressed in

the latest fashions, and handsome young men who would ask me to dance!' She thought about what it would be like to dance at the ball and tears came to her eyes.

She reminded herself that she only had one dress and that it was ragged and dirty.

'Who would even think of inviting a tatty scullery maid like me to a ball at the palace?' she murmured bitterly. She burst into tears at

this desolate thought and buried her face in her hands. Her future looked very bleak and this made her feel even more desperate.

Just then her godmother happened to be passing by and saw Cinderella crying. She came into the house and asked Cinderella what was wrong.

'I would like ... I would like ...' began Cinderella, but she was crying so hard that she could not continue. Her godmother, who was a fairy, guessed what she was trying to say.

'You want to go to the ball too, don't you?' she said.

'Yes,' sighed Cinderella.

'Well, dry your tears and trust in me,' said her fairy godmother. 'First you must go into the garden and fetch me the finest pumpkin you can find.'

Cinderella was intrigued. 'How can a pumpkin help me go to the ball?' she wondered. But she did as she was told and fetched her fairy godmother the biggest pumpkin she could find. Her fairy godmother scooped the middle out of the pumpkin, then she tapped the hollow rind with her magic wand and to Cinderella's great surprise a magnificent golden coach appeared.

Next the fairy godmother asked for the mouse cage. She took six mice out of it and changed them into a team of six magnificent dapple grey horses. Then she took a rat from the rat cage and six lizards she found behind the watering can and transformed them into a big coachman with a moustache and six footmen to ride at the back of the coach.

Cinderella had never seen anything so wonderful in all her life and was struck speechless by her godmother's magic powers.

'There,' said her fairy godmother. 'There is everything you need to go to the ball. Does that make you feel happier?'

'Yes,' replied Cinderella, 'But how can I go to the ball in these awful clothes?'

Her fairy godmother tapped her lightly with her magic wand and in a twinkling Cinderella's dirty rags became a magnificent dress embroidered with gold and silver thread and studded with precious stones. And for her feet Cinderella had the prettiest pair of dainty glass slippers.

Cinderella combed her hair and fastened it up with a simple tiara that matched her dress, then she powdered her face. Her eyes shone so brightly that she did not need to wear any make-up. She looked beautiful enough just as she was.

She was just about to climb into her coach, when her fairy godmother laid a hand on her arm.

'Whatever happens,' she warned Cinderella, 'make sure you leave the palace before midnight because my magic powers vanish then and the coach, your dapple grey horses, the coachman and footmen and your beautiful dress will be turned back into a pumpkin, mice, lizards and rags. The glass slippers will be all you have left, as I am

giving them to you as a present for your first ball.'

Cinderella promised to do as her godmother said then, overjoyed and unable to wait a minute longer, she cried to the coachman,

'Quick, quick, to the royal palace!' and the horses galloped away towards the bright lights of the ball.

When the coach arrived at the palace the valets who were receiving the guests rushed to tell the prince that a beautiful princess had just arrived and that no-one knew who she was.

'She is far more elegant than any of the guests at the ball,' they whispered to him, 'but she looks so modest and unaffected.'

The prince hurried to greet Cinderella and was dazzled by her beauty and her magnificent dress. He helped her down from her coach and led her to the ballroom, unable to take his eyes off her.

A great silence fell when they entered the ballroom. The orchestra stopped playing and all the dancers stood still where they were, because everyone wanted to look at the ravishing stranger. The

17

waiters stopped serving, the stewards forgot to announce the newcomers and the musicians sat with their mouths wide open. Even the prettiest ladies of the court could not help admiring the young girl.

'Isn't she beautiful,' they murmured. 'What a wonderful dress, what lovely golden hair! Hasn't she a good figure! How graceful she is!'

They looked very carefully at her dress and hairstyle so that they could copy her themselves, if they were lucky enough to find material fine enough and dressmakers and hairdressers skilled enough.

Even the king, who was very old, could not take his eyes off her and remarked quietly to the queen that it was a long time since he had seen anyone so beautiful, charming and elegant.

The prince asked Cinderella to dance and she danced so gracefully that the court's admiration for her grew even more.

Everyone sat down to a marvellous feast, but the prince was so spellbound by the beautiful stranger that he could not eat a thing. Cinderella then sat down next to her two sisters and chatted to them in the most friendly way, but they did not recognise her at all. They were very flattered by her attention however and vowed to tell all their friends about it – and Cinderella, to make her jealous.

The evening went by as if in a dream and the time fled by, especially for Cinderella, who was trying to memorise every detail of her marvellous adventure.

All of a sudden the clock chimed a quarter to twelve, so Cinderella made a deep curtsey to the court and left as quickly as she could. It was lucky that she did, because on the way home she turned back into poor, ragged Cinderella with no beautiful dress and no coach and horses at all.

When she was home, she thanked her fairy godmother and asked her if she could go to the ball the next day, as the prince had invited her. Her fairy godmother said yes straightaway. Cinderella had just finished telling her what happened at the ball, when the two sisters came home in a state of great excitement. They were both talking at once, eager to tell Cinderella all about the marvellous time they had had at the ball.

Cinderella opened the door to them.

'You're very late home,' she yawned, rubbing her eyes and stretching, as if she had just been asleep, although she had not had a

moment to rest since she had last seen them.

'You wouldn't have been so bored if you had been at the ball,' said one of the sisters. 'There was the most beautiful princess there whom no-one knew. She was absolutely charming to us and offered us some sweets.'

Cinderella found it hard not to laugh and went so far as to ask what the princess was called. They told her that nobody knew her name and that the prince had been so spellbound by her that he would give anything to find out who she was.

Cinderella was delighted to hear what a good impression she had made on the prince and was very pleased she had left before he could find out her name.

'How I'd like to see this beauty too!' she said naughtily, 'You're so lucky! Sister, please lend me your old yellow dress so that I can come to tomorrow's ball with you.'

'Really my dear, what a nerve!' replied her sister snootily. 'Me lend my yellow dress to scruffy Cinderella, never!'

This was the answer Cinderella had expected and she was perfectly happy because she knew that she *could* go to the ball despite her sisters' unkindness.

The next day, as soon as the sisters had left for the ball, Cinderella set off too, in her fine, golden coach. She was even more magnificently dressed than the day before. The prince was enchanted to see her again. He did not leave her side for the whole evening and paid her endless compliments.

Cinderella enjoyed herself so much that she forgot her godmother's warning. She thought it was about eleven o'clock when suddenly the first stroke of midnight chimed. Panic-stricken, Cinderella sprang to her feet and fled from the palace as quickly as she could. She was in such a hurry that she lost one of her glass slippers on the stairs and did not even notice.

The prince was so surprised by Cinderella's sudden departure that he could not move for a moment. Then his senses returned to him and he ran after Cinderella, but she was already well ahead of him and he could not catch up with her. He questioned the guards at the palace gates but they told him that the only person they had seen go by was a very scruffy servant girl.

Cinderella reached home very out of breath. She had no coach or footmen and was dressed in her rags and tatters once more. The only thing left to remind her of her glory was the second little glass slipper, identical to the one she had lost. She carefully put it away in a cupboard.

When the two sisters came home from the ball, Cinderella asked

them whether they had had a good time and if the beautiful princess had been there again. They said that the princess had been there, but that she had fled suddenly at the stroke of midnight and lost one of her pretty glass slippers in her hurry. The prince had picked it up and had spent the rest of the evening looking at it, unaware of what was going on around him or of the pretty ladies left at the ball. He had obviously fallen deeply in love with the beautiful owner of the little glass slipper.

22

It was true that the young prince could not forget the beautiful stranger who had made such a strong impression on him. How could he ever find her again when he did not know her name or where she lived? He was so desolate at the thought that he might never see her again that he eventually asked his father, the old king, what to do. The king understood very well what his beloved son was going through. He wanted to please him and make him happy, so he thought long and hard about the problem. Suddenly he had an idea. All they had to do was make every young girl in the kingdom try on the slipper, so they could find out whose foot it fitted.

He ordered his prime minister to announce throughout the land that his son would marry the girl whose foot was small enough to fit the glass slipper. Heralds were despatched to the far corners of the kingdom.

The prince was in such a hurry to find the beautiful princess again that he decided to visit each and every young girl in the kingdom himself, to make them try on the glass slipper. The whole country was thrown into a turmoil when the news was announced. Every girl wanted to look her best and took the greatest trouble with her clothes and hair, secretly hoping that the little slipper might fit her.

The prince visited all the princesses, duchesses, daughters of noblemen and the ladies of the court, but without success.

Next he visited the daughters of all the lords and wealthy landowners, but none of them could even fit their toes into the slipper, no matter how hard they tried, and the prince left many shattered hopes behind him.

Eventually he visited the two ugly sisters. They did their best to squeeze their feet into the slipper, but without success, much to their regret.

The prince felt very downhearted and was about to give up and go away, when Cinderella went up to him, her face all smudged with cinders, and asked if she could try on the slipper. She had watched what was happening, had recognised the slipper and had finally plucked up the courage to show herself. Her sisters were indignant at the very idea that such a dainty slipper might fit a grubby scullery maid. They were furious with Cinderella for having the nerve to go up to the prince and speak to him. They were so ashamed of her that they shook with rage. Not for a moment did they suspect what was going to happen next.

The prince was surprised by Cinderella's request, but something about her gentle voice reminded him of the voice he loved, so he granted her request, without much hope. He made Cinderella sit down and to everyone's amazement she slipped her foot into the little glass sliper with no difficulty at all.

Then Cinderella took the other slipper out of her pocket and slipped it on to her other foot, blushing with pleasure.

The prince was overjoyed to find his loved one again at last and recognised her despite her rags. The two ugly sisters could hardly contain their rage at first, but soon they calmed down, deciding it was best to be on Cinderella's side, and immediately became very sweet and charming.

Suddenly the fairy godmother reappeared. She waved her magic wand and transformed Cinderella's rags into the dazzling dress she had worn at the ball. The prince now knew for sure that he had not made a mistake and was beside himself with joy.

Without further delay, he sent messengers to the far corners of the kingdom to announce the good news. As soon as everyone knew about it, they began to prepare for the wedding, which promised to be the most lavish ever.

Lords and ladies came from the neighbouring lands, accompanied by their retinues and bearing presents, each one more magnificent than the last. Everyone wished to give the best present! The whole

kingdom hummed with activity as everyone rushed around preparing for the wedding festivities.

People could talk of nothing but what they should wear, how they should do their hair and how to decorate their coaches and horses. Spinners, weavers, lacemakers, dressmakers and saddlers were summoned and had to work all day and all night. Platforms were

erected in every square throughout the land so that the people could dance on the wedding night.

Red carpets were laid along the streets between the royal palace and the Cathedral. All the houses along the route were freshly repainted, and the church was decorated with thousands of beautiful flowers. Soon, the whole town was bright with colour.

At last, the long-awaited day arrived. Crowds gathered in the streets; the Royal Guard fired a thunderous twenty-one gun salute from the walls of the palace. The bells were ringing from every church in the city as the first guests arrived: the kings of neighbouring lands, ambassadors, lords and noblemen, each one more splendidly dressed than the last. Their ladies were just as elegant. Their gowns were made of the finest fabrics, glistening with pearls, diamonds and other precious jewels.

At last the prince and his bride appeared, followed by bridesmaids and pages who were carrying Cinderella's long train. This was the most impressive sight of all. The cheers doubled in volume and everyone agreed that the prince had made a perfect choice. Cinderella looked very beautiful and radiantly happy. She only had eyes for her husband-to-be. He was magnificently dressed in a costume of midnight blue velvet with a short cape flung proudly over one shoulder, and he was carrying a hat edged with white swansdown. Everyone agreed that they made a fine couple and wished them every happiness.

Nor did Cinderella forget her sisters and stepmother in the general excitement. She was as kind as she was beautiful and forgave them for being so horrible to her in the past. She only made them promise to try and be kind to others in future. Not long afterwards Cinderella introduced her sisters to two noblemen at the court who soon proposed to them, because the sisters were now so charming that no-one noticed how ugly they were any more.

The Brothers Grimm's
SNOW WHITE

Retold by Claude Lanssade

One winter's day long ago a queen was sitting at her window sewing, when she pricked her finger and drew a drop of blood. 'Ah,' sighed the queen, 'how I would like to have a little girl with lips as red as that drop of blood, with skin as white as the snow falling outside and with hair as black as the ebony my chair is made of.'

Not long afterwards the queen's dream came true. She gave birth to a very pretty baby girl and named her Snow White.

The king and queen were overjoyed by the birth of their baby and held grand celebrations for her christening.

The queen's wish

came true and the baby princess was very beautiful. She had skin as white as snow, thick black hair and scarlet lips.

Sadly the queen died soon after the birth. The king was desolate but it was not long before he married again. The new queen was beautiful, but she was very jealous of the little princess's looks and could not bear to have her within sight.

So the little princess was sent away from the court and was brought up by a servant in a remote wing of the castle.

The princess was happy, even though she rarely saw her father, but one day, alas, he died too. Everyone forgot about Snow White,

but as the years went by she became more and more beautiful and graceful.

Now the queen had a magic mirror, which she had inherited from her godmother, who was a witch, and every morning she asked the mirror the same question,

'Mirror, mirror on the wall, who is the fairest of them all?'

And the mirror always gave the same answer,

'You are the fairest, your Majesty.'

Fifteen years went by and the queen led an exciting life while the little princess grew up quietly, far from the hustle and bustle of the court.

Then one morning the queen went to her faithful mirror and asked

it the usual question and it replied,

'You are very beautiful of course, your Majesty, but Snow White is more beautiful still.' For the magic mirror could not lie. The queen was mad with rage when she heard this and summoned one of her gamekeepers.

'John,' she said haughtily, 'Take Snow White deep into the forest and kill her. And bring me back her heart to prove that you have done as I asked.'

The gamekeeper was horrified and protested.

'Be quiet!' snapped the queen. 'Do as I say or I will have you thrown into prison and you will spend the rest of your days there!'

The gamekeeper knew her threats were not to be taken lightly. So the next day he told Snow White that they were going to pick mushrooms and he led her deep into the heart of the forest. The princess was thrilled to be going on an unexpected walk and chattered non-stop to her guide. She gathered flowers and nuts along the way and shared them with him, and as the day went by the gamekeeper felt less and less like carrying out the wicked queen's command. He waited until evening then he suddenly stopped in a clearing and drew out his dagger.

'What are you doing?' asked Snow White innocently. 'Why have you raised your dagger?'

'Your wicked stepmother ordered me to kill you, gentle princess,' said the gamekeeper, 'But I haven't the heart to do as she says. Run away quickly so that she can't find you. And make sure you don't come back to the castle.'

The gamekeeper caught a young deer and cut out its heart to take back to the queen, and Snow White fled into the forest, stumbling with fatigue and fright. She did not know which way to go and night was already falling. It was the first time she had been in the forest on her own and everything looked very fierce and frightening. Wings brushed against her, twisted roots appeared beneath her feet and she tripped time and time again. Snow White ran until her heart was pounding fit to burst, but she dared not stop.

She carried on running for a long time, then collapsed out of breath on a soft, grassy bank in a clearing. When her eyes had grown used to the dark, she looked around her and saw to her despair that she had come right back to the place that she had started from. She had been going round in circles for hours. 'I must keep going,' she said to herself, 'I am far too close to the castle here. The queen is much too clever to believe the gamekeeper's story for long. She will send out a search party for me and I won't be able to escape. What will become of me?'

Snow White rested for a while, to try and regain her strength. She was unaware of all the tiny eyes peeping anxiously at her from behind the bushes.

'I know who it is,' said Mopsy, the rabbit, waggling her long ears. 'It's the little princess from the castle. When I used to raid her nurse's vegetable plot, I often saw her sitting on an old stone bench beneath the tower where she lived, doing her sewing.'

'A princess! A real one!' whispered a wide-eyed fawn in amazement. 'But what's she doing all by herself in the forest in the dead of night? We must take her back to her nurse at the castle. She must be absolutely dying of fright, poor thing.'

'Twit twoo,' hooted an owl, blinking his yellow eyes. 'I will lead her there because I can find any path, even in the dark. Let's wake her up.'

'Wait a minute,' said the rabbit, smoothing her whiskers. 'Yesterday evening I was nibbling a few sprigs of herbs beneath the walnut tree when I overheard a gamekeeper telling a rather nasty story. The queen had ordered him to kill Snow White because she was too pretty. The kind-hearted gamekeeper spared her life, but she has to find somewhere safe to hide so that her stepmother really believes she has gone for ever.'

'Let's think,' said the owl, ruffling his feathers.

'Poor little thing,' said the fawn, his big eyes filling with tears. 'I know,' he cried suddenly, bouncing up and down, 'she should go to the seven dwarfs' house. My mother used to take me there when the huntsmen were combing the forest. The house is far away, hidden behind the mountain. No-one would ever know the princess was there.'

'What a good idea, my friend,' said the owl. 'The dwarfs are said to be kind and they are sure to give this lovely girl shelter. But how shall we tell her which way to go without frightening her?'

'I can do it,' said a pretty robin. 'The princess likes birds. She used to feed us.'

He gently brushed his wing against Snow White's cheek as she lay sleeping, and she opened her eyes and sat up. Then the robin flew on to the branch of a nearby tree and began to sing. Snow White smiled, even though she was feeling miserable.

'I recognise you,' she said. 'You're the cheeky little thing who used to come right up to the table to pick up the crumbs when I was eating. What are you trying to tell me?'

The robin trilled, then fluttered a few metres further away and

started to sing again. He did this several times, moving further away from the clearing each time.

'Ah,' said Snow White, 'I understand. You want me to get up and follow you.'

'Tweet, tweet,' whistled the robin and flew along just in front of her.

Snow White knew that the birds loved her because she had fed them and looked after them during the long, cold winters, and she knew she could trust the robin to show her the way. She followed him for a long time and gradually day began to dawn, lighting up the path before her and chasing away the frightening shadows. She found her little friend's company reassuring, even though he was so small, and she noticed that there were lots of friendly little creatures in the bushes all around her who were too shy to show themselves. One moment a handful of freshly gathered nuts appeared on the path in front of her and another time a rabbit showed her where to find a spring of fresh water.

These refreshments gave Snow White the strength to keep going and a few hours later she caught sight of a wisp of smoke rising from the chimney of the strangest little house she had ever seen.

The robin was very pleased with himself. He flew up on to the roof of the house and sang at the top of his voice.

'I'm here at last,' thought Snow White and she knocked on the door. There was no reply, so she pushed the door open and went inside. To her great surprise she found herself in a small room full of tiny furniture, where everything was in the most terrible mess.

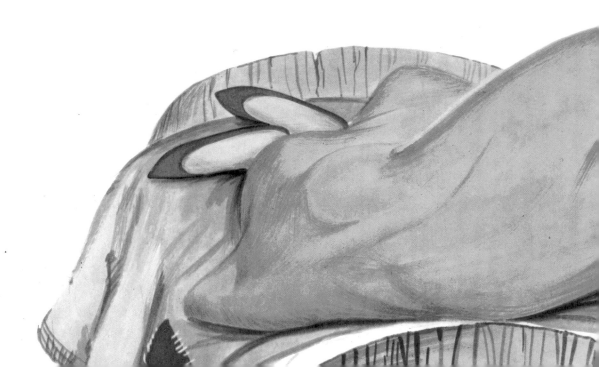

A long, low table was laid
ready for dinner and each place
was set. Snow White counted
seven little bowls, seven minia-
ture goblets and seven sets of
knives and forks small enough
for dolls. There was a wonderful
smell wafting up from a huge
iron pot sitting on the coals in
the fireplace and Snow White
sniffed hungrily.

'I'm sure that whoever lives
here won't mind if I help myself
to a little bit of their dinner,' she
said to herself. 'They must be
kind people or the robin would

not have brought me here, I feel quite sure.'

So Snow White helped herself to some food, then she climbed the dusty stairs and lay down on one of the seven tiny beds which were lined up in a row in the bedroom. She wanted to stay awake until her unknown hosts came home, but she was worn out from her long walk and soon fell asleep.

If Snow White had still been awake she would have heard seven

voices singing a lively song in the distance. The song grew louder and louder, for the seven dwarfs who lived in the little house were coming home after a day's work in the mine. When they entered the house, one of them cried out loudly, 'Who has pushed my chair back and who has been eating from my bowl?'

'Someone has been tasting the stew and has been upstairs,' grumbled another dwarf.

'Let's go and see if there is anyone in our bedroom,' cried the seven dwarfs all together, looking a bit frightened.

They scrambled upstairs, jostling each other, and anxiously pushed the bedroom door open.

'Look, there's the culprit!' squeaked the smallest dwarf in amazement. He went over to shake Snow White and wake her up, but he stopped suddenly, 'Isn't she beautiful!' he murmured in admiration. Snow White did look pretty, with her long black hair spread out over her shoulders, her clear, white skin and her rosy cheeks. But even while she was sleeping she kept sighing, as if she was in some terrible danger.

The other six dwarfs were touched by the sight. 'She *is* beautiful,' they whispered, one after the other, 'but doesn't she look sad?'

Their voices woke Snow White up. When she saw the seven kind little faces looking sympathetically down at her she knew she was in a safe place and told them her sad story. As soon as she had finished, the dwarfs all began to speak at once.

'What a wicked queen!'

'Poor little thing ... you deserve to be happy for a change ... in some quiet, out-of-the-way place where your evil stepmother would never think of looking for you.'

'I've just had an idea!'

'Me too!'

'Me too! I bet we've all had the same brilliant idea!'

And the seven dwarfs joyfully suggested that Snow White stay and live with them in their little wooden house, as it was deep in the wildest part of the forest and no-one ever went there.

Snow White was delighted and clapped her hands.

'I will look after your house for you,' she promised them.

So Snow White stayed in the little, thatched house tucked away beneath the branches of the forest trees, safe from the wicked queen. Every morning the seven dwarfs set off to work in the diamond mine on the mountainside. Before they left they always gave Snow White strict instructions on what she should and shouldn't do.

'Beware of strangers, my child,' the oldest dwarf would say, tugging anxiously at his beard, 'Don't let anyone come into the house.'

'And don't set foot outside the clearing,' Bashful would say, blushing bright red.

Snow White would do her best to reassure them, then she would busily set about the housework. The cottage had never looked so clean. The windows sparkled and the furniture smelt of beeswax. The little dwarfs had clean, well-darned clothes and every evening they would hurry home from work, singing cheerfully, to the delicious meal Snow White had waiting for them.

Nor did Snow White neglect her little friends, the birds. Every morning the warblers, robins and finches would sit outside the front door and sing at the tops of their voices, and Snow White would laughingly throw them all sorts of tasty seeds and scraps of bread. When she was cooking, her little friend and the guide, the robin, would perch on her shoulder so that he could keep an eye on what she was doing.

Snow White liked singing with the birds as she bustled round the kitchen and the forest creatures listened admiringly to her lovely voice.

But no matter how much she sang or tried to amuse herself, Snow White found the days very long and she missed the company of her dear old nurse. The dwarfs did their best to keep her entertained. They were fine musicians and every Sunday they would pick up their instruments and play her traditional songs and dances. Snow White would pick up her skirts and invite one of the dwarfs to dance.

Meanwhile, back at the palace, the wicked queen lived happily, convinced that she was the most beautiful woman in the land. One day, however, she decided to consult her magic mirror once again.

'You are very beautiful, of course,' the mirror said to her, 'but Snow White, who is hiding in the seven dwarfs' house, is even more beautiful than you.'

The queen flew into a terrible rage when she heard this and she prepared to take her revenge. She dressed up in dirty old rags and disguised herself to look old and ugly, then she picked a magnificent apple from her orchard and injected some powerful poison into it.

Disguised as a poor, old hunchback, she set off into the forest and made her way to the dwarfs' house. She knocked at the door, but

Snow White did not answer, so the old 'beggarwoman' called out pleadingly,

'I am dying of thirst, my child, and it is so hot that I think I'm going to faint. Please take pity on me and fetch me a glass of water.'

Moved by the old woman's distress, Snow White forgot the dwarfs' warnings. She opened the door and asked the old woman to come in and sit down, then she gave her a big glass of chilled water.

'This is delicious,' croaked the old woman. 'Look, take this apple by way of thanks. I picked it in my garden this morning but it is too crunchy for my old teeth.'

Snow White took the juicy apple trustingly but no sooner had she taken a bite of it than she fell to the ground in a swoon. The wicked queen was delighted.

'Ha ha!' she cackled, 'Now I am the most beautiful in the land again!' And she fled in the highest of spirits.

The little robin had been watching helplessly from the window ledge. He flew as fast as he could to the seven dwarfs. As soon as they heard him chirping at the entrance of the mine, they knew that something terrible had happened and rushed home. They were overcome with despair when they saw Snow White and tried to revive her, but without success.

'We shall build her a glass coffin,' the dwarfs decided tearfully, 'then we will be able to go and look at her every day. We shall lay beautiful flowers all around her.'

The dwarfs did what they had said and every day for months they went faithfully to visit Snow White. Then one day a prince came riding by as they were kneeling around the glass coffin.

'Why are you crying?' asked the young man curiously. 'And who is that beautiful girl lying among the flowers?'

'It is Snow White, my lord,' said the oldest dwarf respectfully. Just as the prince spoke, his horse accidentally kicked the glass side of the coffin and it broke. The piece of poisoned apple fell out of Snow White's mouth and she opened her eyes.

'We shall be happy together,' she said, as if it were the most natural thing in the world. The prince lifted her up on to his horse in front of him and they set off for his kingdom, followed by the seven dwarfs.

The prince and Snow White were married amidst great celebrations, which went on for a whole two months. The wicked queen choked with rage and died when she heard the news, so the prince and Snow White lived happily together for ever after.

C.L.Collodi's
PINOCCHIO

One fine winter's evening, a fine oak branch which the wind had broken off rolled to the door of the carpenter's shop where Mr. Cherry and his partner, Gepetto, were hard at work.

'Now there's a fine piece of wood!' cried Mr. Cherry when he saw the branch. 'It's just what I need. Sturdy, a good colour and plenty of sap. Come here, little log. This sharp tool will soon turn you into a fine milking stool.'

'Have pity on me,' begged the poor piece of wood, frightened by the look of the sharp tools. 'Look at all the knots I have! You couldn't make anything very special out of me. Make me into a milking stool if you like, but I will be so lumpy that no farmgirl would want me.'

'Give it to me,' said old Gepetto. 'I'll make it into a fine puppet and he can keep us company during the long winter evenings.' So the piece of wood was cut into pieces and carved into a charming puppet by the craftsman's skilled hands. Gepetto made a smooth, round ball for its head and gave it a rascally, pointed nose. Then he carefully painted two bright, beady eyes on it and the brightest red mouth you could imagine.

Gepetto was very proud of his handiwork. He carefully made the hinges for the puppet's limbs, then he sat him down on the workbench.

'Look, master!' he said. 'I shall call him Pinocchio! Look, he is already trying to move and speak. I have always wanted a little boy! I'll have some clothes made for him at once and I'll teach him how to talk.'

So every day Gepetto spent hours patiently teaching the puppet, and it quickly learnt to walk and run like other little boys.

'Now I will take you to school,' Gepetto announced proudly one day.

How pleased Pinocchio was to be able to go to school with all the other children! He laid his exercise book carefully down on his desk and did his best to pay attention.

Suddenly a brass band started to play outside. All the way down the high street you could hear nothing but the blaring of trumpets and the clashing of cymbals, and the sound carried right up into the classroom.

'It's the circus,' whispered the children to each other. 'There are jugglers and a big bear, a puppet master and an elephant.'

'A puppet master,' thought Pinocchio, with excitement. 'I could become the star of his show! What a wonderful career!'

He managed to slip away from school at break time and introduced himself to the puppet master.

'Hmm,' muttered the puppet master slily. 'A fine lot you know about the profession. Those clothes you are wearing are not at all suitable for a beggar, which is the role you will be playing, so take them off at once. And make me an omelette, because I am starving hungry!'

Pinocchio was mortified, but he lit the fire, deep in thought about all the grand roles in store for him. Alas, he was so carried away by his daydreaming that he soon smelt something burning. He had forgotten about the omelette!

'Get out of my sight, you good-for-nothing!' growled the puppet master. 'Pick up your clothes and go and look for your fortune somewhere else. But here, take these five gold pieces. Make good use of them and you won't starve to death!'

Blushing with shame, Pinocchio hurried away, clutching his meagre fortune in his hand. All of a sudden a sugary voice called out.

'Hello, friend. Are you looking for somewhere to stay?'

There, in front of Pinocchio, stood a very strange cat and a very strange fox. They looked so odd that they gave poor Pinocchio a terrible fright at first.

'He . . . hello, gentlemen,' he stammered. 'I don't know where to spend the night, but I have five gold pieces here. I would like to find an inn of good repute because I might be robbed if I went somewhere bad.'

'My good friend,' yapped the fox, 'you are wise to be so cautious. I have fought in many distant lands and have known many famous people, and believe me, common sense is the highest of virtues.'

Modesty was definitely not one of Pinocchio's strong points. He believed everything anyone told him, and these kind words dispelled all his doubts.

'Gentlemen,' he said with a bow, 'I place my fate entirely in your hands. Please will you do me the honour of being my guests at dinner at whichever inn you like.'

His offer was quickly accepted and the three new friends went into the village to look for a suitable inn.

'Here's just the place,' said the cat before long, smoothing his whiskers. 'You can smell the roast meat cooking all the way down the street. Master William, the landlord is known for his cooking throughout the capital.'

'I won't be able to eat much,' sighed the fox. 'All my military campaigns have ruined my stomach. Our young friend will have to excuse me if I just pick at the odd thing or two.'

The dining room of the inn was deserted that evening, but there was some succulent-looking poultry and game roasting on spits in the fireplace.

Master William greeted the three comrades most civilly and told one of the cook's boys to lay the table. In no time at all dishes appeared, one after the other, on the rustic tablecloth. Pinocchio was worried. There were slices of pork and beef, roast chickens and whole sides of venison, iced pastries and cakes and dusty flagons of wine.

'That's far too much,' whimpered Pinocchio with fright.

'Don't you worry about a thing, my friend,' sneered the fox. 'Master William will charge us a very reasonable price as long as we do justice to his cooking. Just look at that chicken! My mouth is watering already! Let's not disappoint our good chef. Your very good health, my friends!'

Pinocchio could not help noticing how the sight of the feast had miraculously revived the fox's appetite. He devoured everything within paw's reach. The cat was more choosy about what he ate and sat twirling his whiskers, but he did manage to drink his way through a vast quantity of wine. Pinocchio himself had a very sweet tooth and could not resist the mouthwatering fruit tarts, nor the gooey nougat. Before long, his stomach heavy from all the sweet things he had eaten, and dazed from having had his glass of wine constantly topped up by the generous cat, he laid his head on his arms and was soon fast asleep.

Without a moment's delay, the two comrades quickly dragged him out to a nearby shed so that they could rob him.

The cold night air woke Pinocchio up and he was overcome with fright when he saw the two robbers leaning over him with sacks over their heads. He let out a great shriek and took to his heels. The cat and the fox were close behind him, but luckily they were slowed down by their disguises.

The unfortunate puppet headed for the nearby forest as fast as he could, hoping to lose his angry pursuers amongst the dark undergrowth.

'How stupid and ungrateful I have been,' he whimpered repentantly. 'My poor father must be so unhappy, thanks to me. If I manage to escape from these robbers, I will go back to him as soon as I can and I will buy him a fine new jacket. But for now I must be careful. I'll hide the gold pieces in my mouth, so that I don't lose them.'

Just as Pinocchio was putting the money in his mouth, the moon appeared from behind a cloud and lit up a majestic castle standing in the middle of a clearing. Pinocchio stopped in amazement for a moment, then ran towards the castle.

'Catch him!' yelped a voice behind him. 'He's hiding the money under his tongue.'

'Let's hang him!' cried the other robber angrily. 'That will make him open his mouth and we'll get the money easily.'

'Help, help!' whimpered Pinocchio and beat his fists against the door of the castle. He could hear his enemies close behind him. High up in the castle a casement window opened and a charming lady looked out.

She was so beautiful, but so strange, that Pinocchio was struck speechless for a few precious moments. For the young lady had long,

blue hair.

Alas, the two robbers had crossed the clearing in the meantime. They seized Pinocchio and brutally strung him up on the branch of a nearby oak tree, hoping that this would make it easier for them to steal his money.

The unfortunate puppet soon lost consciousness, but just as he did, the door of the castle opened and a couple of servants came rushing over to rescue him.

He was carried unconscious to a beautiful little bedroom and there he was looked after by the strange princess with blue hair.

For many days and many nights poor Pinocchio tossed and turned with a fever. Then one fine morning he opened his eyes at last and saw the princess with the blue hair keeping watch over him.

'You're awake at last,' she said in a musical voice. 'I am a fairy and I have been looking after you for many nights now. Here is a drink I have made for you. It will make you strong again, but unfortunately it cannot help make you any wiser.'

'I don't want a drink,' said Pinocchio sulkily. 'I had a drink right at the beginning of all this and that's what made me ill,' he added cheekily.

The moment he told his lie, this nose grew enormously long.

'That is what happens to children who tell lies and don't do as they are told,' said the fairy calmly.

'Please give me a drink. I want a drink,' begged Pinocchio in horror, looking at himself in the mirror. 'Thank goodness my poor Papa can't see me now.'

The fairy lightly clicked her fingers and twelve green woodpeckers immediately flew down and perched on the crestfallen little puppet's enormous nose. They pecked sharply away at it and before long they had reduced it to its normal size.

Pinocchio gradually got better. He had a peaceful time in the fairy's palace, but he was bored and missed his friends, the little village boys.

'I can see that you're tired of being shut up here,' said the fairy to him one day. 'Off you go. Make sure that you are always kind to others and beware of being vain or lazy.'

Pinocchio thanked her and went on his way again, clutching the five precious gold pieces in his hand.

Alas, when he went back to his old friends in the village, they

made fun of him and threw stones at him.

'You ungrateful, lazy thing,' they shouted, 'You broke old Gepetto's heart and he went away soon after you ran off.' So Gepetto, the kind old carpenter, the father who had loved him so dearly, had disappeared all because of him!

Feeling very downhearted. Pinocchio went on his way again.

Suddenly a cart full of children overtook him.

'Look at the handsome puppet, Lucignolo,' they cried to their young driver. 'Let's take him with us. He can join in the show.'

'We are going to the fair,' they explained to Pinocchio, 'because we have formed our own circus and we are going to put it on in the

village square. You can dance with us!'

Pinocchio was quite glad to climb up into the cart. 'After all,' he said to himself, 'I can show what a good dancer I am and who knows? I might come across my dear Papa looking for me.'

The children rode through the town, waving a banner which said,

THE CIRCUS LULU PRESENTS
ITS SINGERS
ITS YOUNG ACTORS
AND PINOCCHIO,
ITS TALENTED DANCER.

Pinocchio had forgotten the fairy's warning and was bursting with vanity. Alas, when the other children were dressing up in their fine costumes he suddenly found that he had grown a horrible pair of donkey's ears.

Pinocchio was very embarrassed.

'I look ridiculous like this,' he whined. 'You said that I would be the star of the show and now the audience will just make fun of me.'

'You know, Pinocchio, it takes a great deal of talent to make people laugh,' said Lucignolo patiently. 'I will dress up in a pair of donkey's ears too and we will do a comic scene. Both of us will dance and you can throw a big bowl of water at me.' This made Pinocchio feel a bit better, so he agreed to dance.

The show soon began and the clowns, the tightrope walkers, the bareback riders and the bear trainer all finished their acts to tumultuous applause. The atmosphere went completely to Pinocchio's head and made him feel giddy. When his turn eventually came round, he went out into the arena, followed by Lucignolo, who was carrying the bowl of water.

The music started to play and Pinocchio began to dance and twirl gracefully around the bowl of water.

All of a sudden he caught sight of the fairy with the blue hair. She was sitting, smiling, right in the front row. Poor Pinocchio forgot what he was doing and missed a step. Then he jumped right into the bowl of water and splashed the flabbergasted audience.

'You clumsy fool,' growled Lucignolo. 'You have ruined the whole scene. I'll tell the lion tamer to throw you out!'

Humiliated and blinded by tears, Pinocchio sadly set off again, throught the moonlit fields and woods. After a few hours he began to feel tired and lay down to sleep on a grassy bank. He was woken up by the rumbling sound of a coach crossing a bridge.

The local coach, pulled by eight donkeys in pink blankets, was trundling peacefully along with the coachman snoring at the reins.

'Wake up, wake up!' called Pinocchio. 'Are you heading for the sea? Please will you take me with you?'

'Well really,' grumbled a donkey, shaking Pinocchio off. 'You complained about having ears like ours and said we were stupid creatures, and now you are asking us to help you! Well this is what we do to rude people like you!' And he kicked Pinocchio into the neighbouring field.

Battered and bruised, and soaking wet from the dew, Pinocchio wept bitterly.

'Dear fairy,' he sobbed, 'Please come and help me. I am so sorry I have been so thoughtless and I promise I will be good at school and work hard from now on.'

No sooner had he finished speaking, than a large wood pigeon flew down close to him.

'The fairy has heard your request and believes that you mean what you say,' cooed the bird. 'We know that Gepetto went to the coast to look for you. Climb on to my right wing and I will take you to a little fishing village. There you can wait for him to come back and in the meantime you can go to school, as you have promised.'

62

Pinocchio climbed on to the bird's back and snuggled down among the soft feathers, with his arms tightly round the bird's neck. The bird soared gracefully up into the sky and flew for two whole hours, then he put his passenger down in a little village.

'Here you are,' said the bird. 'The school must be nearby, because I can hear the bell calling the children back to class. Goodbye Pinocchio. Remember your promise.'

The teacher seemed to be expecting Pinocchio. He made him sit down at a little desk of polished wood, right at the front of the class, and the lesson began.

For many days Pinocchio worked harder than any of the other children. When he wasn't at school, he lived with the teacher in the quiet little flat above the classroom.

But every day, at teatime, Pinocchio went down to the beach, in the hope of seeing Gepetto's little boat on the horizon.

One day Pinocchio was chased by a dog and jumped into the water to escape. Alas, he was as light as a feather and was swiftly carried far away from the shore. Buffeted by the waves, Pinocchio struggled to keep his head above water.

But a whale was swimming nearby. This enormous animal was always hungry and swallowed everything it came across. Pinocchio was sucked into the whale's jaws with a mouthful of water and was thrown into the whale's stomach.

The whale's stomach was like an enormous dark cave. Yet right at the far end of it Pinocchio could see a tiny glimmer of light. Intrigued and hopeful, he made his way towards it. He had to crawl because he was constantly thrown from side to side as the whale swam along.

You will never guess what Pinocchio found! There, at an old seaman's chest lit by a flickering candle, sat old Gepetto.

He was thrilled to see his beloved son again, and for a few

moments they forgot all about the danger they were in. They hugged each other and jumped up and down for joy. They made so much commotion that the whale was annoyed and opened his jaws wide so that he could get rid of this undesirable and troublesome supper.

Pinocchio and his father were delighted and rushed towards the opening.

'Alas,' moaned Gepetto, 'I am too old and I can't swim very well. You will have to go on without me, my son.' But Pinocchio would not listen to him and made Gepetto climb on to his back. He swam like this for a long time until he was exhausted, then he suddenly thought of asking the fairy with blue hair for help.

'Dear fairy,' he cried, 'please come and help us, I beg of you!'

At that very moment a big tunny fish sped towards them.

'Climb on to my back,' said the friendly fish, 'and I will take you to land.'

Pinocchio and Gepetto clambered on to the kind fish's back. Poor Gepetto was chilled to the bone. He clung on for dear life.

Eventually they came to some rocks and knew that land was near. Before long Pinocchio and Gepetto could step ashore. Pinocchio thanked the tunny fish for saving their lives, then he rubbed Gepetto dry with his little jacket.

'Congratulations, Pinocchio. You really do have a kind heart,' said a musical voice. Pinocchio turned round and saw the fairy with blue hair. He threw himself into her arms and thanked her profusely.

'Dear fairy,' he said at last, 'I have another favour to ask of you. I must find a job so that I can earn a living, because dear Papa is too old.'

'That's very good of you,' smiled the fairy. 'Do you see that roof over there? It is a farm. Go there and the farmer will give you work.' With these words, she vanished. Pinocchio and Gepetto went to the farm and the farmer employed the little puppet straight away.

Pinocchio worked hard all winter long. When spring came he set off for the town, clutching all his savings in his hand. He wanted to buy old Gepetto a new jacket. On the way he met a sad snail, who told him that the fairy with blue hair was ill and dying in the town hospital. Pinocchio was very upset.

'I must go there at once,' he cried, 'I have all my earnings with me and shall buy her all the medicines she needs!'

And at that very instant, to his great surprise, Pinocchio turned into a real little boy, and in the distance he could hear the gentle voice of the fairy murmuring,

'When naughty children mend their ways and are good, their most secret wishes come true. How happy Gepetto will be!"

Hans Christian Andersen's
THE
LITTLE MERMAID

Retold by Françoise Chapelon
English Translation by Angela Wilkes

Once upon a time, in the deepest depths of the ocean, there was a magnificent castle built of lilac coral, shimmering mother-of-pearl and sparkling seashells, and in it lived the old king of the sea. The old king had five charming daughters, little mermaids, and each one was as beautiful as her sisters. They had long, blonde, wavy hair which rippled like seaweed, eyes as fine and clear as water and slender bodies which tapered into beautiful fishtails.

The five little mermaids were as charming as they were beautiful. They were gentle and easygoing, but they were also lively and seemed to enjoy themselves whatever they did. Their father loved them all equally but he was sometimes perplexed by his youngest daughter, because she was a little different from her

sisters. She seemed to day dream more and to be less aware of the world around her. The king had given each of his daughters a little garden, and the four older sisters planted theirs with all sorts of seaweed, flowers and underwater plants. The little mermaid, however, had sown hers with thousands of bright yellow seashells, which made it look like the magnificent sun which shone over the land, and which she had never seen. In the centre of this seashell sun stood a pretty white marble statue she had found in a wrecked ship on the ocean bed, during one of her solitary swims. The statue was of a handsome young man, a human who lived on land.

Whilst her sisters were playing with their friends, or were busy looking for shells and pearls for their jewellery, or picking seaweed of unusual shapes and colours to make into pictures, the little mermaid spent whole days in her garden. She would stare pensively at the white marble statue and daydream about the strange kind of life that people must lead up there on land. Their life was a complete mystery

to her and she tried very hard to imagine what it was like.

'What are you thinking about, and why aren't you swimming with your sisters?' the old king asked her, surprised to see her so still and quiet all the time.

'I'm thinking how nice it would be to live on the wonderful land, where the sun shines, like a human being,' said the little mermaid.

'Don't fool yourself,' said the king. 'The climate on land isn't nearly as pleasant as ours. Here the weather is always calm; up there it is sometimes very hot and sometimes very cold, and people have to protect themselves against the bad weather. The people who live on land have to earn their daily bread by working hard. In our kingdom there is plenty of food for everyone and we don't have to fight each other in order to survive. Do you understand?'

'But if I went there,' said the little mermaid, 'I might make some friends.'

'You little fool,' cried the king angrily, 'Humans don't want to meet mermaids. They think them ugly because they have fishtails instead of legs and are different from them. I forbid you to even think such nonsense!'

Despite his words, the little mermaid could not stop thinking about the world of humans. She found their forbidden world both

facinating and alluring, as forbidden things always are.

There was a tradition among the dwellers of the deeps that when a mermaid reached her fifteenth birthday, she was allowed to swim to the surface of the waves for the very first time.

The four older sisters brought back such glowing reports of this eagerly awaited experience that the little mermaid could hardly wait for her turn. She listened to their stories with fascination. They told her they had seen enormous ships ploughing through stormy waves, and magnificent cities on land where thousands of humans lived.

The little mermaid was dazzled by these stories. Life on land was so different – more difficult perhaps, but far more exciting than the life she led under the sea. She was more and more eager to meet human beings and find out how they lived.

She started to spend all her time daydreaming in front of the statue in her little garden. She gave up all the pastimes she used to share with her sisters and just wanted to be on her own. She thought constantly about all the marvellous things her sisters had told her and they fired her imagination even further. She desperately wanted to get to know the strange world up on land and could hardly wait for her birthday.

When the longed-for day arrived, she quickly left the palace without saying goodbye to her father or her sisters, and swam upwards towards the surface of the waves.

She was drawn towards the surface as if by a magnet and swam as hard as she could, so

that she would not lose a single precious moment.

It was night when she reached the surface, and a terrible thunderstorm was raging. There were great gusts of wind, and heavy, black clouds were scudding low over the mountainous waves which were breaking with a deafening roar. Flashes of lightning rent the sky and you could hear the muffled rumble of thunder above the noise of the waves. It all looked very frightening to the little mermaid, who was used to the peace and quiet of the watery deeps, but she managed to swim quite easily in spite of the rough seas and just dived through the waves when they were too big. She swam like a fish and neither the currents nor whirlpools could stop her from reaching the coast, so that she could see the land and the people who lived on it at last. She was very tired, but she was now so close to her goal that she could not give up.

Suddenly, through the driving rain, she saw the shadowy mass of a magnificent ship which had struck a reef and gone down, with all aboard.

Then all of a sudden a flash of lightning lit up some wreckage drifting nearby, and on it the little mermaid saw a young man. He was unconscious and badly wounded, and was about to be engulfed by the mighty waves breaking all around him.

'I must save him!' cried the little mermaid. Without thinking of the danger, she swam towards him as fast as she could. She lifted him up and struggled bravely through the surf to dry land. She dragged the young man out of the water and laid him down gently on a deserted little beach.

The young man was pale and very cold and looked as if he was dying. The little mermaid was worn out, but nevertheless she looked after him with tenderness and devotion all night long. She could not take her eyes off his delicate face and thought how much he looked like the marble statue in her little garden.

'How handsome he is!' she thought sadly. 'If only I could spend the rest of my days with him. Alas, it is impossible.'

When the sun rose and it began to get warmer, the young man started to look a bit better, but he still did not regain consciousness.

All of a sudden, a pretty, well-dressed young girl came walking down the path to the beach. The little mermaid was frightened and hid behind a rock, and she saw the stranger bend over the young man, then call for help.

The little mermaid was relieved to know that the young man she had rescued would be safe, but she was sad to leave him so soon. She dived into the sea, which was now calm again, and swam back to the underwater kingdom of her father, who was waiting anxiously for

his daughter's safe return.

From that day onwards, the little mermaid thought constantly about the young man whose life she had saved. She spent hours sitting alone in her little garden, daydreaming. Sometimes, in the hope of hearing news of the young man, she would swim back to the beach and hide behind a fishing boat or a rock, so that she could listen to the fishermen talking.

In this way the little mermaid found out that the handsome young man was none other than the reigning prince of the land, and that he lived not far away in a splendid palace overlooking the sea.

She also heard the fishermen say how the pretty young girl had found the prince lying unconscious on the beach and had had him carried back to his palace so that he could be looked after. When he regained consciousness and had wanted to thank the young girl, he found she had gone away without being able to say who she was or where she came from, because she was a foreigner and spoke a different language from the prince. Nobody mentioned the little mermaid because no-one had seen her rescue the prince. They only talked about the beautiful stranger whose courageous act had saved their beloved prince, and she was praised by all the people in the kingdom.

Every time the little mermaid came back from one of her trips to the beach, she looked more and more downcast and unhappy. Her father and sisters were so worried about her that her father finally said to her,

'Tell me what is upsetting you, my child. You know that I would do everything in my power to help you. Your sisters and I love you and we only want to see you happy.'

The old king spoke so kindly and tenderly that the little mermaid could contain herself no longer. She burst into tears and poured out her heart.

'Dear father, I know that what I am about to say will hurt and disappoint you, but I want to go back to the land and join the handsome human prince whom I love, so that I can marry him, if he will have me.'

The old king was very taken aback.

'So you want to leave your family and your magnificent home?' he cried. 'But my poor child, this human prince will never fall in love with a mermaid! You are a daughter of the sea and you are quite different from him.'

'I have heard that there is a witch who lives in the underwater grotto not far from your castle,' replied the little mermaid, 'and she knows how to make a magic potion which can transform mermaids into women. Once I look like a normal woman I will be able to make the prince love me. Please, father, let me go and see the witch!'

The little mermaid seemed so hopeful and determined that at last her father sadly gave her his permission to do as she wanted. He spent a long time deep in thought before he was able to accept that one of his daughters was going to leave him for good, because he foresaw all the difficulties that might lie ahead of her. His heart filled with pain and bitterness just to think of it. He had dearly wished to end his long life peacefully amongst his own kind, in his marvellous palace surrounded by all his loved ones.

However, the little mermaid did not hesitate. As soon as he had given his permission, she hurried to the frightening grotto where the horrible witch lived.

The witch sneered when she saw the little mermaid. 'I can tell from your sad eyes what's brought you here, you little fool,' she said. 'I warn you, you will have to pay dearly for the magic potion which will turn you into a woman.'

'It cannot be too much for the pleasure of spending your whole life with the one you love,' said the little mermaid. 'What do you want of me in exchange for your precious potion?'

'You must give me your wonderful voice,' hissed the witch, 'the voice which charms all those who hear it.'

The little mermaid shivered. She remembered the happy days when she and her sisters had sung together so wonderfully that all the deep sea creatures had come hurrying to listen to them. However, her love and determination were so strong that she did not hesitate for long.

'I will give you my voice,' she murmured, 'but please make your potion quickly.'

'First let me take my payment,' muttered the witch.

She went over to the little mermaid and chanted a few mysterious words, making magic signs as she did so. When the little mermaid tried to speak, not a sound came from her lips. She was dumb for evermore. Now she realised what she had done, but the hope of being able to walk like a human being just made her determination all the stronger.

The witch was busy for three long hours. It seemed like an eternity to the poor little mermaid. The dreadful old woman pounded together toads, snakes and other hideous monsters that were creeping round about, until finally she had a transparent potion, which she poured into a crystal flask.

'Take this flask,' she said to the little mermaid. 'You must drink the potion just as the sun is setting and it will turn your beautiful fishtail into two human legs. But think carefully about it first, because during the transformation and then afterwards at every step

you take, you will feel an intense pain. And remember that whatever happens, once you are a woman, you will never be able to turn back into a mermaid again. Think carefully about it!'

The little mermaid grabbed the flask eagerly, without hesitating, and hugged it to her.

'What does it matter that I lose my voice or have to suffer pain, as long as I am close to the one I love,' she thought. And without looking back or stopping at her father's palace, she swam straight to the beach and lay down on the sand. When the sun sank below the horizon she swallowed the witch's dreadful potion.

The drink had an immediate effect; the little mermaid was in such terrible pain that she fainted. Night fell . . .

When the little mermaid regained consciousness she had two slim, pretty legs instead of her fishtail, and to her surprise the handsome prince was bending over her, looking down at her with the greatest kindness and concern.

'I found you unconscious on the sand as I was going for a walk,' he said. 'Have you been in a shipwreck? Where do you come from? What is your name?' He was very surprised that she didn't answer his questions.

The little mermaid made signs to show him that she was dumb. Feeling sorry for her, the prince helped her to her feet and took her to his palace over-looking the sea. During the short walk the poor little mermaid very

nearly collapsed, as a stabbing pain shot through her with every step she took. But bravely she did not show that anything was wrong and no-one would ever have known how much it hurt her to walk. By sheer strength of will, she managed to walk gracefully like a normal woman, and to keep smiling.

84

The prince was delighted by her grace and delicacy and gave her a charming apartment of her own in his palace, pretty clothes to wear and everything she needed to make her life enjoyable. He also taught her to dance, so that she could entertain him in his leisure time.

From then on the little mermaid lived close to her beloved prince and he made sure that she had a good time, whilst he enjoyed her pleasant company. She accompanied him on his long horse rides, shared his pastimes, played the harp to him and went to the theatre with him, but she was bitterly sorry that she could not sing him the songs she had learnt as a child and charm him with her beautiful voice.

Her life could have carried on in this peaceful and contented way for a long time, but the young girl was not happy. The prince felt nothing more than a warm friendship towards her, because his heart belonged to another young girl, the one he had seen when he opened his eyes after the shipwreck. He could not forget that face . . .

'I cannot stop thinking about the beautiful stranger who saved my life when my ship went aground,' he would say to the little mermaid sometimes. Then, without realising the pain he was causing, he would continue,

'But my beautiful stranger went away without being able to tell me who she was or where she lived. I have looked everywhere for her since then, but I haven't found her. I feel as if I will never be able to love anyone else.'

The little mermaid wanted to cry when she heard this. If she had been able to speak, she would have told the prince that it was her and her alone who had saved him from the storm and who had looked after him all night long. But alas, she was dumb, and the prince would never know that he owed her his life.

Time passed. Then one day the prince had his finest ship rigged out so that he could pay a visit to the king of a neighbouring island. He took his charming little dancer with him, to entertain his guests during the crossing.

The voyage passed without incident. All the passengers were cheerful, but impatient to reach their destination and get to know the island and the people who lived there. The minute the prince disembarked, he was led to the king of the island.

And what should he see, to his surprise! Next to the royal throne stood the king's daughter and it was none other than the beautiful stranger he had been seeking for so long!

He joyfully begged the king to give him his daughter's hand in marriage. The king was delighted to entrust him with the happiness of his beloved child, so the two were married and there were great celebrations. Shortly afterwards the young couple returned to the prince's land aboard his ship.

The little mermaid felt bitterly sad. She looked sorrowfully at the sea. Ever since she had forsaken her ocean have to live on the land, she had experienced nothing but pain, bitterness and disappointment.

Suddenly she saw her sisters swimming after the ship and waving to attract her attention. Full of hope, she leant over the ship's rail to hear what they had to say.

'The witch has promised to turn you back into a mermaid if you kill the prince before daybreak,' they cried, throwing her a dagger. 'Do it quickly.'

The little mermaid hesitated, then she grabbed the dagger and crept into the prince's room. She bent over him as he lay asleep with his young wife, but he looked so happy that she hadn't the heart to kill him. She tossed the dagger into the waves, then she threw herself into the sea. As she did so, she heard a chorus of hundreds of voices calling to her, 'We are the daughters of the air and it is our job to comfort those in sorrow. Come with us.'

At once the little mermaid felt comforted and happy. She soared upwards into the welcoming arms of her new friends, to begin another, better life with them.

The Brothers Grimm's

HANSEL
And
GRETEL

Retold by Claire Laury
English Translation by Angela Wilkes

Long ago there lived a poor woodcutter. His first wife had died and his second wife was a hard-hearted woman who did not love her stepchildren, Hansel and Gretel. They all lived in a humble cottage deep in the forest and the woodcutter worked very hard, yet he scarcely earned enough money to feed his family and this made his wife very angry. One year there was a terrible famine throughout the land and so one evening the whole family had to go to bed without having had anything to eat.

'Don't worry,' said the woodcutter's wife to her weeping husband, 'all you have to do is take your children deep into the forest and leave them there. Once they are on their own, they will have to look after themselves.'

At first the woodcutter was indignant and refused to do it. But his wife managed to persuade him that kind people would look after the children, so he finally consented to do as she wanted. Now Hansel, the boy, was still awake, because he was hungry, and he heard everything his parents said. So when they had gone to sleep he crept silently out of the house and down to the banks of a nearby stream. He filled his pockets with white pebbles, then went back to bed and calmly went to sleep.

Early the next morning the woodcutter's wife woke up the children.

'You have slept for long enough, you lazy things,' she said. 'Get up and come with us. We are going to gather firewood.'

Hansel and Gretel did as they were told. For a long, long time they followed their parents until they were deep in a part of the forest that they did not know. They felt so tired that they were stumbling at every step they took.

When they came to a clearing the woodcutter's wife stopped and, pretending to feel sorry for the children, she built a big bonfire for them.

90

'Warm yourselves up and go to sleep, while your father and I gather wood,' she said. 'We will come back and get you when we have finished.'

When their parents had gone, the children lay down close to the fire. They were so tired that they soon fell fast asleep.

When they woke up it was night-time and they were all on their own. Gretel was very frightened and ran to and fro calling her parents. When there was no reply, she burst into tears.

'Don't worry, little sister,' said Hansel calmly, 'we will just go home.'

'But how will we find the way?' sobbed Gretel. 'It is so dark and we don't know where we are.'

'Last night I heard our stepmother plotting to leave us behind,' replied Hansel, 'so I made a plan.'

'What plan?' asked Gretel in astonishment.

'I will explain,' said Hansel, 'but first dry your tears. We must set off at once.'

As the two children marched briskly through the woods, Hansel told Gretel how he had secretly collected the white pebbles from the bank of the stream the night before and how that morning he had scattered them all the way along the path into the forest, without his stepmother noticing. So now the white pebbles would help them find their way back to their father's cottage.

'What a clever idea!' cried Gretel, hugging Hansel joyfully. So the children found their way through the tall trees. They were helped by the moon shining in the starry sky, which lit up the white pebbles Hansel had scattered along the ground.

Towards daybreak they finally came in sight of the woodcutter's cottage and rushed towards the door, which had been left ajar.

'Papa, Papa, we're back!' they shouted, as they ran joyfully into the house. Their parents were astonished to see them.

'My dear little ones,' said the woodcutter, kissing the children tearfully. 'I was paid a good price for the wood we gathered yesterday, so I have bought plenty of food and we no longer have to part. Thank goodness! I was so miserable at having abandoned you!'

So for a while the woodcutter and his family lived happily and had plenty to eat, and the woodcutter's wife had to hide her resentment. But as soon as the food ran out the wicked woman once again persuaded her husband that they would have to abandon the children. Heavy at heart, the weak-willed woodcutter agreed to her wishes.

Yet again Hansel overheard his parents' conversation, but this time the door of the house was locked and he could not go and collect any pebbles. So the next

day, when the woodcutter and his wife led the children into the forest, Hansel scattered little balls of bread along the ground.

When they reached the heart of the forest and the parents went off to gather wood, the children went to sleep without worrying, sure that they would easily find their way back to the cottage, thanks to the little balls of bread that Hansel had scattered along the path. Imagine their horror when they woke up and found that the hungry little birds had eaten all the pieces of bread!

'How shall we ever find our way

back now?' sobbed Gretel. 'What are we going to do?'

'Be brave, little sister, and follow me,' said Hansel. "If we keep walking in a straight line, we are bound to reach the edge of the forest and find some kind people who will take pity on us.'

But the unfortunate children walked all night long and for part of the following day without coming across a living soul or finding a house where they could take shelter.

'What will become of us?' whimpered Gretel. It was beginning to get dark and she was feeling tired, hungry and miserable. Then suddenly something unusual caught her attention.

'Hansel, look at that graceful white bird flying along in front of us,' she said. 'It keeps turning round, as if trying to tell us to follow it.'

'Well let's follow it then,' said Hansel, who was also feeling very tired. 'Perhaps it belongs to someone and will lead us to its master, who might offer us something to eat and a bed for the night.'

When the bird heard this, it chirped cheerfully and flew down a mossy path.

Full of hope, Hansel and Gretel followed the beautiful snow-white bird through the thick forest.

Gradually the path grew wider, then it opened out into a pretty garden full of wild flowers, and in the middle of the garden was an entrancing house. The house was so strange that the children stopped and stared at it in amazement.

'Look, Hansel!' cried Gretel with delight 'The walls of this pretty house are made of nougat, the door and the window frames of crystallised fruit and the window panes of whipped cream!'

'And its roof is made of gingerbread with nuts in it . . . and there are macaroons and sugared almonds on the shutters!' added Hansel, clapping his hands.

The bird had perched on the roof of the house and was singing 'Tweet, tweet.' He seemed to be telling the children to come and feast on all these delicacies.

Hansel and Gretel were so hungry – for they had not eaten since

the morning of the previous day – that they did not need to be pressed and rushed gleefully towards the tasty house. What a treat all these marvellous sweets were!

'This tastes good,' murmured Gretel with her mouth full as she savoured the door handle, which was made of caramel.

Hansel was far too busy eating everything that came to hand to be able to talk!

While the children were having their feast, the white bird flew away and suddenly the door of the house swung open without a sound.

'Enjoy yourselves, children. You seem to like my house a lot!' cried a shrill but friendly voice.

Hansel and Gretel turned round and saw an old woman come out of the strange house and look them up and down with curiosity.

'We beg your pardon,' they stammered, full of confusion.

The old woman laughed mockingly.

'There is no need to make excuses,' she said. 'I am delighted to think that nibbling my house will help to fatten you up a bit because at the moment you are far too skinny for my liking!' Then she added kindly, 'You look very tired, my dears. Come and have a proper meal, then you can spend the night here.'

Delighted by this unexpected offer, Hansel and Gretel spent a happy evening in the strange little house. They ate a huge and delicious meal, then they went to bed in a comfortable little room and had the sweetest of dreams.

But the next day, just as they were thanking their new friend for being so kind, she pushed Hansel into a dreadful cage and locked the door.

Then she turned to the terrified Gretel and shouted nastily, 'As for you, little fool, from today onwards you will be my servant. Woe betide you if you don't work from morning to night, or if you try to set your brother free, because I am going to feed him up for a few weeks and when he is fat enough I will invite other witches like me to come and help me eat him!'

Yes, the old woman who had seemed so friendly the day before was really one of those wicked witches who tempt little children to their houses so that they can eat them!

Gretel trembled when she heard the wicked witch's terrible threats. But she held back her tears and resolved at once to do everything she could to set Hansel free as quickly as possible and to run away with him. Several days went by, however, before she had the chance to put her plans into action.

In the meantime Hansel was bored to tears in his dreary cage. His only pleasure was eating, because the wicked witch fed him delicious food. You could almost see him growing fatter, much to the delight of the sly old woman.

'Well done, my boy,' she cackled cruelly, 'Just a few more weeks of this diet and we will be able to eat you. Then it will be your sister's turn!'

She never suspected that meek little Gretel was waiting night and day for the moment when she could take her revenge. Her opportunity finally came one morning when the witch had told her to light the oven and get lunch ready.

When the oven was hot, Gretel called her mistress and asked her innocently to come and see if they should add some logs to the fire. Then when the unsuspecting witch leant over the flames Gretel gave her an almighty shove into the oven and shut the door on her.

'There, you cruel, wicked witch!' she cried. 'That's what you deserve for putting us through this ordeal!' Then she grabbed the old woman's keys and ran to set Hansel free. She threw her arms round her brother's neck, weeping for joy.

'Quick,' he cried, 'we must get

away quickly and escape from that terrible old woman!'

Then Gretel told him what had happened to the witch.

'There's nothing to be afraid of,' she said. 'She can't do us any more harm. In fact now she can do us a great service.'

'What do you mean?' asked Hansel.

'Well,' replied Gretel, 'since I've been here I have often noticed the witch go and lock herself in the attic and there I heard her counting out her treasure. Let's go and look for it quickly because I am sure it will be very useful to us.'

The children found a magnificent hoard of treasure in the witch's attic and they filled their pockets with gold and silver coins. Then, not wishing to spend a moment longer in the place where they had come so close to death, they fled without a single backward glance.

Hansel and Gretel ran straight through the forest for a long time and they did not stop until they came to a vast lake surrounded by wooded hills. Worn out, Gretel collapsed on the grass and looked anxiously at the lake.

'Where is Papa's cottage?' she asked, beginning to cry.

'It must be on the other side of the lake,' said Hansel, suddenly feeling calmer, 'but how shall we ever get across it?'

No sooner had he spoken than a majestic swan who was swimming peacefully nearby came gliding up to them and looked at them in such a gentle and friendly way that they trusted him at once.

'He wants to give us a ride,' said Hansel, 'Let's go!'

So Hansel and Gretel climbed onto the swan's back, and as soon as they were sitting comfortably he set off across the water, carefully avoiding the rocks and banks of reeds.

The journey lasted for about an hour and when the swan reached the opposite shore of the lake he stopped in an inlet, so that the children could jump ashore more easily.

But before Hansel and Gretel had the chance to thank their friend and say goodbye, the magnificent bird had vanished. He was a magic swan and had to go to the rescue of other children in need.

Kind-hearted Gretel was sad and blew a farewell kiss after their feathered friend.

Soon after they had left the lake the children came in sight of their father's cottage and rushed towards it.

'We've brought you back some treasure!' they shouted. 'From now on we shall never have to be apart and we will always have enough to eat!'

The woodcutter welcomed his children back with open arms and even his horrible wife was sorry for what she had done and was pleased to see them. So they all lived happily together for ever after.

Jonathan Swift's

GULLIVER'S TRAVELS

Retold by Françoise Chapelon
English Translation by Angela Wilkes

One fine day in May 1699 Gulliver, a citizen of London, set sail from Bristol on the good ship Antelope. Gulliver was tired of his dull life in England and wanted to try his fortune in the South Seas.

For a long time the voyage went well, but at the beginning of November the Antelope was caught in a violent storm somewhere off the East Indies. The sailors fought hard to save the ship, but the storm was too fierce. The Antelope was hurled on to rocks and a huge hole was torn in her side. Within minutes she began to sink.

Gulliver, with five of the ship's crew, managed to scramble into a lifeboat. Hoping to find an island where they could land, they rowed with all their strength.

The hours passed. Lashed by wind and waves, the sailors grew too weary to row any further and slumped over their oars. Suddenly, SMASH! A mighty wave hit the little boat and overturned it. Gulliver and his friends were flung into the sea. Fortunately Gulliver was a strong swimmer and he managed to keep himself afloat. He soon lost sight of his companions amid the towering waves, but he swam on bravely.

'I must keep going,' he thought with fright as he felt himself weakening. 'If only the storm would die down! If only I could reach land and find some people living there!'

Suddenly, far away on the horizon, he caught sight of an island he had never seen before and full of hope he swam towards it. At last he reached it and staggered ashore.

'Safe at last!' he cried. Exhausted and streaming with water, he looked all around him.

To his disappointment there was no sign whatsoever of any

habitation. He was trembling with cold and felt he could go no
further.

Still, he took his courage in both hands and stumbled onwards
through the rocks and across the barren, windswept beach.

'Is anyone there?' he shouted from time to time. 'Isn't there anyone who could help a shipwrecked sailor? I am worn out and starving hungry!'

But no-one answered his calls, so he carried on, stumbling with fatigue at every step he took.

After about an hour he came to a beach of fine sand. It was dark by now so he sank to the ground and fell into a deep and dreamless sleep.

He slept for nine hours and when he finally woke up he saw that the storm had passed and the sun was shining from a clear, blue sky. The air was warm and sweet and his clothes were completely dry. He could hear a murmuring sound nearby, then he heard tiny cries and silvery laughs.

'So I'm not on a desert island after all,' thought Gulliver with delight. 'What a stroke of luck! Someone is obviously coming to help me.'

He tried to get up, but to his great surprise he could not move. He could not raise himself onto his elbows or bend his knees or even turn his head.

'What on earth has happened to me?' thought Gulliver anxiously. He wondered at first if he was dreaming, but then he sneezed loudly and realised he must be awake, so he tried to look around him to see what was going on.

It was then that he saw he was tied down. His hair, arms, body, legs and feet were all tied with ropes as fine as the threads of a spider's web and these were fixed to the ground with miniscule stakes. Gulliver was held well and truly prisoner.

'This joke has gone far enough!' he cried impatiently, upon which hundreds of shrill little voices yelled in his ears, 'What's the matter, giant? Aren't you comfortable?' Gulliver looked to see where the voices were coming from. To his amazement he saw lots of tiny people no bigger than his hand bustling all round him.

'Who are you and where am I?' he asked.

'You are in the kingdom of Lilliput and we are its people,' came the answer.

'Why have you tied me up like this?' asked Gulliver.

'Because our emperor said that we must not let an extraordinary visitor like you go until he had seen you with his own eyes,' replied the little people.

Once the tiny people saw that Gulliver was gentle and would not hurt them, they became quite friendly. They brought him two barrels of wine to drink – each one held barely a mouthful for Gulliver. Then, seeing that their huge guest was hungry, they sent a

116

wagon to collect bread from all the bakers nearby so that Gulliver could have a meal.

Despite his bonds Gulliver began to like this land of midgets and wanted to find out more about it.

'If I promise not to run away,' he said, 'will you set me free so that I can go and pay my respects to your emperor in person?'

'Of course we will,' came the reply. 'We will cut your ropes with an axe, then we will take you to the emperor and empress. They are longing to meet you!'

Gulliver was the subject of great curiosity and the cause of much general concern on his way from the beach to the palace.

'What a fine-looking man!' cried voices from all sides. 'But watch where you put your enormous feet or you might trample on our houses!'

Gulliver did not dare go inside the emperor's palace for fear of knocking down the roof and walls, but he bowed so graciously to the emperor and empress that they even asked to stand in the

palm of his hand so they could take a closer look at their massive visitor.

Once the polite chat was over the emperor asked Gulliver if he would do him a favour. 'You see, Gulliver,' he explained, 'we have enemies on our neighbouring island, Blefuscu. The people there are the same size as us but there are far more of them and they want to wipe us out. As you are so big and strong I wonder if you would help us to free ourselves of them?'

'You can count on me!' cried Gulliver. 'Give me an hour and I will sort out your enemies!' He headed for the coast, leaping over houses, palaces, streets and gardens on his way, then he strode into the sea and waded towards Blefuscu. Within thirty strides he was in sight of the island. There was a great festival in the main square of the capital that day and all the people of Blefuscu were there, even the sailors from the navy, who had left their ships to go and have some fun with their friends.

'That's lucky,' thought Gulliver. He took from his pockets the tiny ropes with which he had been bound and tied them to the prows of the enemy ships, then he pulled them back to Lilliput behind him. Without their Navy the people of Blefuscu were no longer a threat to the Lilliputians.

A triumphant welcome awaited Gulliver on his return to Lilliput! The emperor wept for joy and the empress nearly fainted with emotion. Everywhere people called out enthusiastically,

'Long live Gulliver! He has saved us from our worst enemies!'

Gulliver was made an honorary citizen of the island and a fortnight of non-stop celebrations was declared, in honour of his victory.

Gulliver was the hero of Lilliput and from then on he could no longer go anywhere on the island without being escorted by a noisy brass band which played a fanfare as he arrived in each new place.

The little people were both affectionate and curious and they smothered Gulliver with attention. They climbed up him to take a closer look at his face and did not leave him a moment's peace. They even pattered to and fro along his shoulders all night long, just to make sure he was sleeping well.

However, Gulliver did not feel at home in Lilliput because nothing was the right size for him. The houses were too small for him to enter, there was no bed big enough for him and if he wanted to eat or drink his fill he had to eat a whole flock of sheep or drink a lake dry.

The situation became so difficult both for the Lilliputians and Gulliver that Gulliver decided to continue on his voyage. He said goodbye to his little friends and promised not to forget them but to come back and visit them one day. Then one fine morning he set off in a southerly direction.

The sea was calm and he walked into it until he was calf-deep. He waded through the waves for a long time, but as he went further the water grew deeper and towards the end of the day he had to swim for several hours. It was getting dark by the time he reached land.

Tired from his long swim, Gulliver walked ashore and came to a wheat field where the stalks of wheat were as thick as tree trunks. Gulliver thought he must already be dreaming, so he lay down beneath one of the giant stalks of wheat and fell fast asleep.

He was woken up by the sound of thunder, then realised that he had been lifted off the ground and was lying on something soft and warm which looked very much like a giant hand.

'Where am I?' he cried in terror.

'In Brobdingnag,' boomed a voice – which he had just mistaken for thunder. 'And I have never seen a person as ridiculously small as you here before. You are no bigger than a mouse and I very nearly trod on you.'

Taken by surprise and more than a little frightened by what was happening to him, Gulliver bowed politely to the giant man, who was holding him gingerly between finger and thumb and who seemed just as surprised as Gulliver himself.

'Don't be frightened,' said the man, 'I will take you home with me. I am a widower but I have a little girl who would love to have a pretty toy like you.' And he stuffed Gulliver into his pocket.

Gulliver found it hard to breathe in the bottom of the man's pocket but he soon forgot his discomfort when he was taken out of the pocket and set down in front of the most enchanting little girl he had ever seen. This was Glumdalclitch, the man's daughter. She was only nine years old but she was already as tall as a house.

'How sweet you are,' she said to Gulliver, smiling kindly at him. From then on Glumdalclitch and Gulliver were the best of friends, even though Glumdalclitch was gigantic and Gulliver only tiny.

The little girl gave Gulliver a doll's house to live in. It was beautifully furnished and contained everything Gulliver could possibly want. At night Gulliver went to sleep in a doll's bed, he wore elegant clothes of braided silk that Glumdalclitch had made specially for him and she cooked delicious meals for him on a tiny stove, which Gulliver then ate from doll's china.

Gulliver was very happy in his doll's house, but every now and then something dangerous happened. One day, for example, a big rat sneaked into the house and looked Gulliver up and down cheekily.

'You're so small, I could eat you in one mouthful!' cried the rat scornfully. But just as he was about to attack Gulliver, Gulliver drew out his sword and thrust it into him, killing him on the spot.

Another time Glumdalclitch had whipped up some delicious cream. Gulliver was keeping watch on the dish when a cat came along, licking its chops, ready to pounce on both the cream and Gulliver.

'Get back!' cried Gulliver and his voice was so fierce that the cat took fright and ran away.

Harvest time came and Glumdalclitch's father's crops were ruined by a storm. He was feeling very sorry for himself, but Glumdalclitch suddenly had a bright idea.

'Surely no-one in the land can ever have seen a person as small or as learned as Gulliver!' she exclaimed. 'If we put him on show at the big fair that is coming to town soon we will make enough money to keep us going until the next harvest!'

So that is what they did. One fine morning the fair came to town and Glumdalclitch put Gulliver on show then called out to the people passing by,

'Come and see, come and see! Gulliver may be very small but his knowledge is vast! He will answer any question and you can pay him whatever you think fit.'

Gulliver looked so handsome in the fine clothes that Glumdalclitch had made for him that everyone stopped to admire him. By the end of the day Glumdalclitch had a purse full of coins and Gulliver was the talk of the whole kingdom. The king and queen of Brobdingnag took a great interest in him and bought him from Glumdalclitch's father for a handsome sum of money.

Glumdalclitch was very sad to part with Gulliver, although she knew that he would be well treated by the king and queen.

'Please don't forget me,' she begged, and Gulliver swore that he would always remember her kindness.

A royal coach took Gulliver to the palace, where the king and queen gave him a warm welcome. They were delighted by his wit and

his polite way of talking, and ordered special quarters to be made for him with a tiny bed, table and chair.

From then on Gulliver lived at the royal court and was much admired by all.

He would have been very happy, only from time to time he had the most terrible adventures. One evening he was attacked by a swarm of wild bees and had great difficulty fighting them off with his sword. Another time he fell head-first into a cup of milk and would certainly have drowned had he not been able to swim.

Then, one day, as Gulliver was taking a walk near the royal zoo, he saw a strange animal leaping from branch to branch among the trees. It was an enormous monkey and it looked very fierce. Gulliver was amused by the monkey's acrobatics and stopped to watch, when suddenly the monkey saw him. It pounced on Gulliver and was about to carry him up into the treetops so it could eat him at leisure.

'Help, help!' cried Gulliver, thinking his time had come. Unfortunately he had dropped his sword in his panic and could no longer defend himself. But his cries were heard by the wardens of the royal park, who immediately sounded the alert. Soldiers came rushing to Gulliver's rescue from all sides. They managed to snatch him from the furious monkey and carried him triumphantly back to the king and

queen, who were very worried.

'What a fright you gave us!' they cried to Gulliver. 'From now on you must not leave the palace. It is the only place where you are safe.'

But Gulliver shook his head.

'No,' he said. 'I don't belong here in Brobdingnag where everything is too big for me any more than I did in Lilliput, where everything was too small. The only place where I will feel at home is my own country, and I want to go back there.'

'Gulliver is right as usual,' said the king, and the queen burst into tears.

The king and queen were very fond of their clever little friend and wanted to make him happy, so they had a tiny boat built for him which contained everything he needed to make his voyage comfortable.

Gulliver set sail one fine summer's day. His heart was heavy as he waved goodbye to his dear friends of Brobdingnag.

The voyage was long but uneventful, and a year later Gulliver sailed into the port of Bristol in England. It was winter and very cold. The sky was grey and it was pouring with rain.

However, Gulliver was in high spirits. At last he was back in his own land with his fellow Englishmen, who spoke the same language, thought about things in the same way and who were neither too big or too small but exactly the same size as him.

Gulliver was greeted with joy by his family, who had given him up for dead when they heard that the Antelope was lost.

'What have you been doing all this time?' his father asked him.

Gulliver began to tell him how the tiny people in Lilliput lived and what the giants on Brobdingnag did, and he enjoyed telling his story so much that he vowed to go back one day and visit both his tiny friends and his giant friends on the other side of the world.

'After all,' he said, when he came to the end of his story, 'what does it matter what size these people are? They are my friends. They like me and I like them.'

THE
THREE
LITTLE PIGS

Once upon a time there were three sweet little jolly pink pigs. One was called Arthur, one Boris and the other one Ben. When the summer holidays came, they said to their mother,

'We would like to build three pretty little houses, one for each of us. You would like that, wouldn't you, Mama? It would make us so happy and we would have such fun!'

'It's an excellent idea, children,' replied their mother, 'but do you know how to build houses? They have to stand up straight and be very strong.'

'Of course, Mama,' said the three little pigs. 'We are big now and of course we know how to build houses. As soon as we each have one of our own, we will invite you to them.'

'Thank you, children. It is very thoughtful of you. I will gladly give you permission to build your little houses, but watch out for the big, bad wolf. People say that he prowls around here, so you must be very careful.'

The mother pig gave each of her sons a freshly baked roll for his tea and the three little pigs thanked her, then went off together. They were talking so excitedly that they did not pay the slightest attention to anything that was going on around them. When they came to a crossroads, they parted company and each of them went his own way.

The carefree little pigs did not notice the big, bad wolf, who was hiding in the bushes and patiently keeping watch on them.

Arthur soon finished his roll as he went on his way. Then he began to hum quietly to himself. Before long he met a farmer carrying some huge bales of hay on his back.

'Hello,' said Arthur, 'My name is Arthur and I would like to build myself a house. Please will you give me some of your hay?'

'Of course I will, Arthur,' said the farmer. 'Take as much as you need and good luck with your house.'

Arthur set to
work at once. He undid
the huge bales, then measured
out the ground to make sure his house
would be square. He got some stakes and
drove them into the ground, then he carefully built
the walls out of hay, leaving an opening for the window
and another one for the door.

'How pleasant my house will be,' he said to himself. 'It will be nice
and warm and I will be really comfortable. I wonder what Mama will
think of it when I show it to her. I'm sure she will be thrilled to have
such a clever son and will be very complimentary. As for the

big bad wolf, if he really does exist and is prowling around here, he will never dare attack me in case I give him a good hiding.'

As he was thinking this, Arthur climbed up his ladder to admire the view from the top of the house. Then, feeling very proud of both himself and his house, he climbed back down and got ready to spend a peaceful night in his pretty little house.

All of a sudden he heard someone at the door.

'Knock, knock. Knock, knock!'

'Who's there?' called Arthur suspiciously.

'Open the door to me, little pig!' cried a voice.

'I don't open my door to strangers,' said Arthur.

'I'm coming in all the same, so bad luck!' came the reply and the wolf – for it was the big bad wolf speaking – huffed and puffed with all his might and blew the house down. Then he pounced on the little pig and gulped him down whole in one mouthful!

In the meantime Boris, one of the other two pigs, had walked for a long time until he met a farmer leading a grey donkey carrying big bundles of sticks.

'Hello,' said Boris. 'My name is Boris and I would like to build myself a house. Please could you give me some sticks?'

'Of course I will, Boris,' said the farmer. 'Just take whatever you need, and good luck with your house.'

Boris thanked the farmer and set to work at once. He undid the bundles of sticks, measured out the ground to make sure his house would be square, drove some stakes into the ground, then wove the sticks together very carefully, making sure he did not scratch himself. He left an opening for the window and last of all he put in a door.

'How pleasant my house will be,' Boris said to himself. 'It will be nice and warm and I will be really comfortable here. I wonder what Mama will think of it when I show it to her. I'm sure she will be

thrilled to have such a clever son and will pay me lots of compliments. As for the big bad wolf, if he really exists and comes prowling around, he will never dare attack me in case I give him a good hiding!'

Boris was very happy and jumped for joy. He had finished his house by evening and was just about to go to bed when he heard someone at the door.

'Knock, knock. Knock, knock.'

'Who's there?' called Boris suspiciously.

'It doesn't matter. Open the door!' came the reply.

Boris was surprised at this.

'I wonder why the stranger at the door won't tell me his name,' he said to himself. 'I'd better be on my guard!'

'I don't open the door to strangers!' he called, feeling more and more suspicious. He quickly piled everything he could find up against the door – sticks, planks, stakes, tools – and he barricaded himself in as well as he could.

But the stranger knocked even harder on the door, as if he was mad, and shouted at the top of his voice,

'Open the door, little pig. I don't want to do you any harm, I promise!'

'Go away!' squealed Boris. 'I won't open the door!'

'For the last time, open the door, or I swear you will be sorry!' came the reply.

'No, a hundred times no!'

'If you don't open the door, I will come in all the same and it will be so much the worse for you!' called the wolf – for it was the big bad wolf outside – and he huffed and puffed and charged against the house. Crash! He knocked it down. The sticks scattered in all directions, the walls collapsed, the stakes were sent flying and the roof came crashing down. Boris was knocked dizzy and rolled on the ground. He was trembling all over and his teeth were chattering.

When the cruel wolf saw the poor little pig, he pounced on him with his jaws wide open and gulped him down whole in a single mouthful.

Then, licking his chops and feeling rather full and drowsy after his hearty meal, he crept away into the woods to have a rest. The big bad wolf spent the night deep in the heart of the woods. When he woke up at daybreak, he remembered that there was a third plump little pink pig somewhere in the neighbourhood. 'He will make me a tasty meal,' said the wolf and set off in search of him.

And what had become of **Ben**, the youngest of the three little pigs? Well, he had met a stonemason.

The stonemason was a tall young man with fair hair and a cap

perched on the back of his head. He was pushing a wheelbarrow piled high with bricks.

'That's just what I need,' thought Ben, so he went up to the stonemason.

'Hello,' he said, 'My name is Ben and I want to build myself a house. Please will you give me some bricks?

'Of course I will, Ben,' said the stonemason. 'Just take what you need, and good luck with your house.'

Ben thanked the kind stonemason and set to work at once. But how do you build a house of bricks?

The little pig thought carefully. He got out his rule and took some measurements to make sure that his house would be square. Then he took out his plumbline to make sure that the walls would be really straight. Finally he laid the bricks in lines, one on top of another, and stuck them firmly together with mortar, leaving large openings for the window and door.

Before finishing his house, Ben looked at it with great satisfaction and rubbed his trotters together.

'How pleasant my little house will be! It will be nice and warm and I will be very comfortable. I wonder what Mama will think of it? I'm sure she will be thrilled to have such a clever son and will be most complimentary. As for the big bad wolf – if he really exists and does come prowling around here – he won't dare attack me in case I give him a good hiding! I am sure I am going to have a wonderful holiday here!'

Ben carried on working on his house until evening. He built the frame of the roof and laid it with tiles. Then he built a chimney, cleaned the inside of the house, tidied away his tools and sat down exhausted.

'Finished at last!' he said.

He shut the door, closed the shutters and happily got ready to have a good night's sleep in his charming little brick house.

It was dark and Ben was just about to go to sleep when all of a sudden he heard someone knocking at the front door.

'I haven't given my address to any of my friends yet,' he thought. 'Someone has come to the wrong house.'

He tried to go back to sleep, but the knocking started again, only louder this time.

'Knock, knock! Knock, knock!'

'Who is it?' called the little pig eventually.

'Open the door at once!' came the reply.

Ben was suspicious when he heard this and called out impatiently,

'I don't open my door to strangers. Go away!'

'If you don't open the door, I will come in all the same and it will be so much the worse for you!' cried the wolf – for it was the big bad wolf again. Then, huffing and puffing, growling and cursing, the wolf hurled himself at the brick house with all his might ... and broke his nose. He whimpered and fell backwards with his paws in the air!

'It's obviously going to be harder this time,' said the crestfallen wolf, picking himself up. 'I shall have to change my tactics.'

He went away and spent the night in the woods, hoping that this would give Ben the chance to forget the unfortunate visit. But the next day as it was getting light he crept stealthily back to Ben's house.

The wolf put on a false, sickly-sweet voice. 'Hello, little pig,' he said in his most friendly way. 'I am your closest neighbour, and as you know neighbours are there to do each other a good turn. So I want to show you the places where you can find fruit and vegetables easily. There is a turnip field on the hill next to Martin's farm. I will come and fetch you at six o'clock if you like, and we can

go and dig up lots of turnips.'

'All right,' said Ben. 'I will expect you at six o'clock.'

The wolf went back into the woods, delighted to think that he would go into the trusting little pig's house at six o'clock and gulp him down in one mouthful. He went to have a rest in the forest in the meantime.

But Ben was more shrewd than his two brothers and he did not trust this big wolf with cruel eyes and a false voice. So, at the beginning of the afternoon, he hurried to Farmer Martin's field and filled a whole basket with big, juicy turnips. Then he galloped back home, locked and bolted his door and cooked the turnips for his dinner.

In the meantime the wolf had a good rest and dreamed about his next meeting with Ben. The very thought of seeing the innocent little pink pig again, pouncing on him and gulping him down, made the wolf drool with pleasure.

The time soon passed and the wolf set off, humming happily to himself. He bounded along the road to the little brick house.

When he got to Ben's house at six o'clock, Ben was eating his turnips and the house was all locked up. No matter how hard the wolf knocked at the door, he could not get in.

The next day the wolf suggested that he take Ben to pick apples in Lucas's orchard at five o'clock. Ben agreed to go, but at four o'clock he set off for the orchard on his own and picked his apples. All of a sudden the wolf appeared.

'So you got here before me, Ben,' he said. 'It doesn't matter though. Come down from the tree and I will help you carry your basket.'

'Not yet,' said Ben. 'I want to pick some more apples. I will throw them down to you and you can pick them up.'

Ben threw the apples so far away that the wolf had to run to pick them up. As quick as a flash, the little pig rushed home and locked and bolted the door.

The wolf was very determined however, so not long afterwards he went back to Ben's house.

'There's a fair in the town tomorrow,' he said. 'We could go there together. I will come and pick you up at three o'clock.'

But Ben still didn't trust the wolf. The next day he went to the fair all on his own, well before three o'clock, and he didn't stop to look at anything.

The little pig hurriedly bought a big wooden churn for making his

butter. He quickly strapped it on to his back and set off for home again as fast as he could.

But what should he see, all of a sudden, at the bottom of the hill? None other than the big bad wolf prowling around!

The wolf had at last realised that Ben was making fun of him and he was prowling the fair, feeling very angry and hungry, saying to himself that if he came across the little pig, he would gulp him down in one mouthful.

But Ben was too clever for him. He curled up in a ball inside his churn and set it rolling fast down the hill, very pleased with the trick he was playing on the wolf.

'It's fun rolling like this,' he thought.

The wolf was terrified by the rumbling noise made by the churn. 'What is that strange cask hurtling towards me?' he thought, trembling with fright. 'It will crush me if I'm not careful.'

When the little pig got to the bottom of the hill, he jumped out of the churn, ran home and locked himself in. The wolf got there a few minutes later.

'Knock, knock. It's three o'clock!' he cried in a sugary voice. 'Open the door at once, little pig, and let's go to the fair.'

'I am sorry, Mr. Wolf,' said Ben, 'I can't open the door because I can't find my key. But if you climb up on to the roof you can slide down the chimney straight into my dining room.'

'All right. I'll be there in two minutes,' said the wolf with delight, thinking he was about to achieve his aim at last.

Then Ben picked up a big cooking pot of boiling water from the stove and carried it over to the fireplace . . . suddenly there was a dull thud, followed by a splash. The wolf had come tumbling down the chimney into the pot of boiling water and drowned!

Then Ben picked up a pair of scissors and cut open the wolf's

149

stomach. Out jumped Arthur and Boris! How pleased the three little pigs were to see each other after their long separation! They hugged each other joyfully and joined hands, singing,

'Let's dance round and round,

For now we are safe and sound!'

Hans Christian Andersen's

THE
LITTLE
MATCH GIRL

Retold by Claude Lanssade

Once upon a time in Denmark there lived a poor little girl whose parents both died. Life was not too difficult for the little girl at first because she had a kind grandmother who looked after her. But unfortunately the good old lady died when the first cold autumn days came, and the little girl was left all on her own in the garret where they had lived together.

The poor child was so unhappy that she fell ill too, and she had to spend what few savings she had on food and medicine.

When at last she was able to go outside again, the cruel winter had come and the icy winds blew straight through her thin clothes. The biting cold made her tiny hands red and sore and her bare feet sank into soft layers of freshly fallen snow. To earn some money, the little girl carried a tray with boxes of matches for sale on it.

'It's Christmas Eve,' she said to herself, 'Surely the passers–by will take pity on me and pay a good price for these boxes of matches. It's easy to do someone a good turn when you are happy and are going home with your arms full of presents.'

'Come and buy my matches so that you can light your candles,' she called out. 'Buy them for your pretty Christmas trees!'

But her frail voice was carried away by the howling wind and the streets stretched deserted before her.

That year, in fact, it was so bitterly cold that the people of Copenhagen had finished their Christmas preparations several weeks earlier than usual and were now staying indoors in the warmth of their homes.

You can imagine the brilliantly lit rooms inside the snowcapped houses, gently heated by enormous tiled stoves. Throughout the town people were getting ready for Christmas while the little match girl wandered despondently through the empty streets, shivering in her ragged clothes.

Occasionally, without much hope, she would stop in front of the heavy, shut doors and call out weakly, 'Who needs matches? Buy my fine matches!' But no-one heard her. Everyone inside was too busy watching the children play with their brand new toys or look for their brightly wrapped presents, lighting the candles on the Christmas trees and eating the delicious goodies spread out on tables laden with flowers, china and silver.

The poor little match girl did not need much imagination to guess

what was going on inside the fine houses. A few years earlier she had led an easy life herself, having been the spoilt daughter of doting parents, and her stocking had always been brimming with wonderful treats on Christmas morning. It tore her heart to think of those carefree days of love and affection. 'If only Grandma were still alive,' thought the little girl sorrowfully, 'We used to have some fun even in our nasty garret. Grandma was good with her hands and used to embroider pretty tablecloths for the rich people and I had no trouble selling my matches because I painted pretty pictures on the matchboxes. What will become of me now? My paintbrushes are worn out and my paints have run out and I haven't a single penny to buy any more. Now no-one wants to buy my boxes of matches.'

156

But the little girl pulled her ragged shawl more tightly round her shoulders and went on her way through the deserted streets, driven on by hunger and the cold.

Several times she thought she saw someone and ran towards them full of hope to offer them her matches. The first time the longed-for customer turned out to be nothing more than a tree swaying in the wind. The second figure she thought she saw at a street corner turned out to be a snowman, rigid beneath its shell of frozen snow and indifferent to her suffering. The little girl turned away in disappointment and was walking away, heavy-hearted, when all of a sudden she saw a man walk quickly by and go up to a house.

With renewed hope, the little match girl began to run. She was as light as a bird and barely left any footprints in the snow.

'Faster, faster,' puffed the little girl to herself, summoning up all her strength.

'Sir,' she called, 'Please be kind and wait for me.' The man was wrapped up warmly in a thick, fur-lined cloak. He turned his head when he heard the little girl, then frowned as she laid her frozen hand pleadingly on his sleeve. He brushed the tearful matchgirl roughly to one side, went into the house and slammed the door behind him.

The little matchgirl sank despondently into a corner. She was chilled to the bone and starving hungry, and curled up to keep warm. The street had gone quiet again and the icy wind continued to blow mercilessly.

The little matchgirl felt herself gradually growing more and more drowsy and struggled to stay awake, for she knew it was dangerous to fall asleep in the snow. Her grandmother had often told her tales of explorers who had lost their way in the Far North. The terrible white sleep overcame them as soon as they stopped, exhausted, to rest for a few minutes and lay down in the soft, powdery snow. The snow would cover them with its treacherous white blanket and they would freeze to death.

'What shall I do? Where shall I go? What will become of me?' the

little orphan asked herself anxiously. It seemed a long, long way back to her garret. Her legs were stiff with cold and she did not feel like going back to the bare, ugly room which reminded her so much of her dear old grandmother. Suddenly an idea came to her. She would use those useless matchboxes with their wet, soggy lids, to keep herself warm. Her fingers were numb with cold and so clumsy that she wasted the first few matches she tried to light.

Weeping with frustration at having wasted her only source of warmth, the matchgirl struck another match against a matchbox. At last she had a flame, a small light flickering timidly in the icy wind.

The little girl held her breath and cupped her hands round the golden flame so that it grew bigger, and shone brightly. 'How wonderful,' she sighed, and indeed the tiny bit of warmth brought a rosy glow to her pale cheeks.

But alas, all too soon the match began to shrivel and smoke, then it went out ... The little girl quickly tried to light another one. Crick, crack! She lit several matches, one after the other. The matches only provided a moment's warmth, but it was enough to revive the weak little girl. The fleeting moments of warmth and light reminded her of the long, hot summers she used to spend at the seaside in the past ... There was the sand close to her, still warm from the day's sun. How soft it felt beneath her bare feet! Everything was bathed in a golden haze of heat. In just a few moments the bell would ring to say that tea was ready and Grandma would put the strawberry tart and the jar of honey on the table ...

The little matchgirl gave a long shiver. The last match in the box had gone out and once again there was nothing but the cold, the dark and that aching loneliness which children hate so much ...

'What a shame a match's flame lasts for such a short time,' sighed the little matchgirl.

Hunched against the wind she counted up her treasure. She only had a few matchboxes left. But the night was so cold and the biting wind so cruel that she felt her resolution waver; she could not bear to go on suffering on her own like this any longer.

Quickly, without any more thought, the little matchgirl lit several matches. Suddenly a large, glowing shape began to form in the flickering light of the flame.

'It's a stove,' murmured the little girl in amazement, 'a wonderful big tiled stove exactly like the one we used to have at home.'

'Yes, it's me, the good old stove from days gone by,' rumbled the stove, shifting from one side to another. 'Don't you recognise my pretty blue trimmings? Come closer, my dear, and take a look at the

glowing red coals inside me. Come here and I will give you the warmth you need so badly.'

Then, like some great friendly animal, the good old stove made a humming sound like a bee, gave a snore loud enough for ten grandfathers, stirred its embers, shook its cinders and blew on the tiniest pieces of coal. Its curved sides turned dark red with all the activity.

'It's going to explode,' thought the little matchgirl anxiously. But just as she opened her mouth to warn the stove of the danger it was in, her last match went out. The icy night closed in on her again and she realised it had all been a dream. Tears of disappointment ran down her cheeks. She was weak with hunger becuase she had eaten nothing for two days except for a crust of dry bread she had found at the back of a cupboard.

Plucking up courage, she went up to the nearest house and knocked at the door. Alas, there was such a din inside the house that no-one heard her timid knocking.

The matchgirl sat down sadly in the corner of the old wall again and resigned herself to seeking comfort from her fast-dwindling supply of matches.

She lit a few more matches, but their warmth only lasted for a few fleeting moments. Then all of a sudden a door swung open right in front of her and she could see into a vast dining room full of gleaming furniture. The lights were dim at first, but then they grew brighter and a huge table appeared. It was covered with a heavy white cloth and laid with sparkling silverware. But it was the rich array of food that most impressed the starving girl – sugary pink and green sweets, cakes and biscuits piled high on silver plates, and glistening golden honeycombs.

The little girl crept up to the sumptuous banquet. There, on a huge

silver platter, sat a magnificent roast turkey with a crackly golden skin. It was streaming with a savoury sauce and encircled with sautéd potatoes. How wonderful it would be to break a wing off this plump bird and to munch some of the potatoes soaking up that tasty sauce!

The girl held out her hand, thinking she could at last satisfy her hunger, but suddenly the matches went out and she was plunged back into the darkness and her despair. The cruel, icy night wrapped its biting breath around her once more and her pangs of hunger seemed to grow even stronger. The little matchgirl sat in a stupor for a few moments, then she decided to light some more matches.

She lit a whole fistful of matches in one go and they crackled merrily, hardly flickering in the wind. Nothing happened at first, then suddenly a huge shape began to form above the ground. The little matchgirl held her breath and an enormous glowing fireplace rose up in front of her. Then streamers appeared from out of the darkness, one by one, and draped themselves across the white marble and over the blackened hearth. Finally a Christmas tree emerged majestically from the wall and took its place in front of the fireplace, its branches bowed down with the weight of its decorations.

Each branch was proudly adorned with gold and silver garlands and with brightly coloured, pearly baubles. Numerous candles flickered amidst the frosted branches and right at the top of the tree gleamed the golden star of Bethlehem, decorated with silver threads. All sorts of colourful parcels full of surprises seemed to be hidden among the boughs and the fresh, invigorating scent of pine wafted all around the tree. Suddenly the tree began to speak in a deep, melodious voice,

'Do you remember, my child, how much you used to admire me when you were little? I stood in your room, looking very proud, but really I was dying of thirst. My needles went yellow and I missed the fresh winds of the forest where I was born. I could feel myself slowly dying in front of that scorching fireplace. You were scarcely more than a baby at the time, yet every evening you took the trouble to water my poor dried up roots. Even before the Christmas celebrations were over, you begged your parents to give me a place in their garden, so I was carefully replanted, thanks to you. Do you remember those hot summer days when you used to come and play with your dolls in the shade of my branches? What are you doing here all on your own and dressed in rags?'

The little matchgirl burst into tears at the thought of her happy past.

'Dear tree, how could I forget you?' she replied. 'You used to bow your branches as I went by, to greet me. Do you remember the violets I planted in the moss at your roots, or the little squirrel which fell through your branches one day? Sometimes, when it was hot, Grandma used to sit beneath you sewing and doze off to sleep. Those were happy days!

'Alas, dear tree, my parents were killed in a storm at sea and our pretty house was sold. Grandma and I spent a few happy months together in a little garret room, but now I am on my own and it is very hard on Christmas Eve. Let me stroke your needles.' But just as the little matchgirl held out her trembling hand to touch the tree, it seemed to melt away and the icy cold night returned, enveloping the girl in its lonely darkness once more.

The little matchgirl wanted to make the beautiful tree from her past come back again, so she quickly lit another handful of matches. The tree quietly reappeared before her and obligingly lowered its boughs, so that its little golden bells rang and flickering flames rose from the multicoloured candles.

The child's eyes shone starrily and her heart swelled with pleasure, but then, to her despair, the tree seemed to slip backwards and it

disappeared from her view once again.

Alas, the little matchgirl had no more matches left, so there was no longer any hope of bringing back the comforting presence of the stove, the tasty meal or the fir tree.

The little matchgirl shrank back into her corner with her back to the hard, freezing cold wall and burst into tears. The glowing dreams she had just had made her actual loneliness seem all the harder to bear. Her body shook with sobs, using up what little strength she had left.

Suddenly she felt something brush against her shoulder and saw an old lady standing in front of her. The old lady's face was deeply lined. She had light blue eyes which looked kindly at the little matchgirl from over a pair of steel spectacles and a warm, generous smile which made her look younger than she really was.

The little girl rubbed her eyes,

'Grandma, is it really you?' she cried joyfully. 'Let me touch you, let me kiss you. You won't go away like the other dreams I've just had, will you?' And she threw herself into her grandmother's arms and tenderly laid her cheek against her grandmother's delicate skin.

The little girl put her thin arms tightly round the neck of her grandmother, who had so miraculously reappeared, and the old lady carefully wrapped the child's frozen feet in the folds of her shawl.

'My dear child,' said the kind old lady, 'I couldn't bear to go on watching you suffer from where I was on the other side of the kingdom of shadows. First I got permission to send you some happy dreams full of childhood memories to cheer you up. By doing this I hoped to comfort you until some kind soul took you into one of these fine houses. But now I can see that no-one will open their door because it is far too cold. No-one will dare venture out on to these windswept streets.

'So listen, dear child, will you come away with me and leave this world behind? We would be together for always but you might miss playing with children of your own age, and the changing of the seasons and the pleasure of having done a lesson well. And you would have to give up hoping that a rich family might adopt you one day. What do you think?'

'Dear Grandma,' murmured the little matchgirl, 'I couldn't bear to lose you again. What have I to go back to? I no longer have the time to go to school because I have to earn my living. You can see how hard that is when the cruel winter is making life so unbearable for me. Surely you don't really want to send me back to that bare garret on my own? Please take me with you. We will be so happy together for always. I am tired of waiting and hoping that people will be kind to me when their happiness has made them blind to the misery of others.'

So the little matchgirl and her grandmother flew away to the land of those who no longer belong to this world, and there they lived happily ever afterwards.

Lewis Carroll's
ALICE
IN
WONDERLAND

Retold by Claude Lanssade
English Translation by Angela Wilkes

'This must be the hottest day of the summer holidays,' thought Alice, as she lay stretched out lazily on the grass in the garden. It was far too hot to do anything.

All of a sudden an extraordinary-looking white rabbit ran close by her. To Alice's surprise, it was smartly dressed in a red waistcoat, and it was actually *talking*. She quite clearly heard him mutter, 'Oh dear, I shall be late, I shall be late.'

Alice was intrigued. She sprang to her feet and went after the strange creature, who was already running away, muttering anxiously to himself, 'By my ears and whiskers, I shall be late.' He scampered behind a bush and suddenly popped down a rabbit-hole. Now Alice had one great fault: she was very curious. So, without a moment's hesitation, she went down the rabbit-hole too. Still, even so she had the time to remark how odd it was that the rabbit-hole was so big. 'Very peculiar,' she thought, as she found herself sliding

faster and faster down the hole, but she wasn't in the least bit worried and had a good look at the vast number of shelves lining the walls of the extraordinary rabbit-hole on her way down. 'Rose petal jam', she read on the label on one of the jars.

'I must be in some kind of larder,' thought Alice. All of a sudden she landed on a thick bed of leaves and moss and found herself at the entrance to a long passageway. The white rabbit was disappearing into the distance. Alice sprang to her feet and ran after him, but the rabbit hurried on, muttering,

'I swear by the tips of my whiskers, the duchess will have me executed if I keep her waiting!'

'Wait for me!' cried Alice, but no matter how fast she ran, she could not catch up with the white rabbit. Soon she found herself all on her own. After a little while she came to a velvet curtain. Alice lifted it and behind it, to her surprise, she found the prettiest, tiniest little door you could imagine. She knelt down and peered through the keyhole and there was the loveliest garden she had ever seen. It was full of green paths and rosebushes, beds of pansies and velvety lawns. Alice wanted to go into the garden at once but the little door was far too small.

Alice was beginning to feel rather sorry for herself when she turned round and saw an elegant glass table, and on it lay a small golden key exactly the right size. Alice opened the door, but still she could not enter the garden because she was ten times too big to fit through the door. 'If only I could shut up like a telescope,' she thought sadly. At that very moment, to her great surprise, a bottle appeared on the little table, and on it was a label saying 'Drink me.' Alice was far too sensible to drink something she didn't know anything about, so she looked carefully at the bottle. There was nothing on it saying 'Poison', so she decided to drink it straight away. The drink was delicious. It tasted like strawberry tart, roast turkey and chocolate ice cream all at once. When Alice had drunk the last drop, she felt a strange sensation creeping over her. 'I'm shrinking!' she thought.

At first she was rather alarmed to see her wish come true so quickly. 'I hope I don't disappear altogether!' she thought. But Alice stopped shrinking when she was about 20 cm tall, much to her relief, and she trotted over to the little door. It was just the right size for her now, but when Alice turned round to get the key she realised that she'd left it on top of the glass table. She tried her best to climb up on to the tall, slippery table, but it was impossible.

All of a sudden, a small, round tin appeared next to the table. On it was written, 'Eat my cakes.' Without a moment's thought, Alice opened the tin and began to munch the cakes. In this strange world, it seemed only natural that she immediately began to grow like a gigantic plant. In no time at all, her head was touching the ceiling. She quickly grabbed the key, then realised that she could not fit through the door any more. I am afraid that at this Alice threw the most terrible tantrum of her life. She stamped her foot and shouted until the walls shook, then she began to cry and flooded the ground with her enormous tears.

'Tip, tap, tip, tap'. The sound of approaching footsteps made her look up. It was the white rabbit. He was wearing a dinner jacket and white gloves and was fanning himself frantically as he hurried along.

'Excuse me, sir,' said Alice timidly. She frightened the white rabbit so much that he jumped backwards, dropping his fan, and ran away, squealing, 'It's an ogre!' Feeling very downhearted, Alice fanned her face, which was all puffy from crying, then all of a sudden she realised that she was shrinking again very fast, so fast in fact that she threw the magic fan as far away from her as she could and rushed happily over to the door, which was once again the right size for her. Then she slipped and fell into a great pool of salt water.

176

'Goodness, it must be the sea,' thought Alice in bewilderment, then she realised it was the pool of tears she had made when she was crying. Alice found the water quite refreshing after all her troubles and began to swim around lazily.

A whole crowd of animals soon came to play in the new swimming pool. There was a fox and a flamingo, a lobster and a hen with her two chicks, a crow, two mice and a squirrel, and more and more animals kept arriving, delighted with this new pool. Alice felt tired, so she got out and sat on the bank, shivering in her wet clothes. All the other bathers faithfully followed her example and sat down next to her, their bedraggled fur and feathers dripping with water.

'We should have a race,' said a mouse, 'so that we don't catch cold.'

'Yes, yes, let's have a race,' cried the other animals, and without waiting for a signal to start they all set off at once, running round and round in circles, jostling and bumping into each other.

Alice was shocked. 'How badly behaved they are,' she thought. 'I've never seen such a badly organised game. But I'll run all the same, so that I warm up.'

The race stopped as soon as everyone was dry and the bizarre competitors began to dance round Alice, demanding prizes. Feeling rather frightened, she fumbled in her pockets and drew out a few sticky sweets. She was pestered from all sides and soon all the sweets were gone. Alice was on the verge of tears when a bright idea came to her.

'My cat, Dinah, is a marvellous hunter,' she said confidingly to the

nearest mouse. 'I sometimes wonder if she isn't really a tiger in disguise. I'm sure that if I called her she'd come and pay me a visit.'

'Look, it's dinner time already,' said the squirrel, creeping away.

'Come along, chicks,' said the mother hen. 'It's time you were in bed.'

'I'll see you soon, Miss Alice,' said the pink flamingo politely, slipping away as quickly as he could.

The cunning little girl laughed to herself when she saw them all leaving. She tidied her hair, then went back to the little door and entered the garden at last.

She walked down a path which was every bit as pretty and shady as she had imagined. All of a sudden she stopped in amazement. There, on top of a mushroom sat an extraordinary blue caterpillar. He was wearing a turban and puffing majestically on a hookah.

'Who are you, my child?' he asked in a deep, musical voice.

'To tell you the truth,' murmured Alice, who was rather confused by everything that was happening, 'I'm not really sure any more because I keep changing size.'

'What a stupid answer,' said the caterpillar. 'Can't you do any better than that?'

'Everything is really very mysterious,' said Alice, trying as hard as she could. 'I'm sure you must know what I mean, because you change from a chrysalis to a caterpillar. It feels most peculiar and is really very worrying.'

'It all seems perfectly normal to me,' said the caterpillar drily. 'What size do you want to be?'

'I want to be big again,' sighed Alice. 'I am far too small at the moment. It's very tiring and I feel as miserable as a worm.'

'What an unkind thing to say,' muttered the caterpillar angrily and glided towards the long grass. Alice was embarrassed and realised she had deeply offended him. Still, as he went away he said,

'Have a taste of the mushrooms. The one on the right will make you grow bigger and the one on the left will make you grow smaller.'

Alice was delighted. She carefully broke off a few pieces of the mushrooms he had told her about and put them in her apron pockets, taking great care not to muddle them up. The pieces in the right pocket would make her bigger and those in the left pocket would make her smaller.

'I must be on my way,' she said to herself cheerfully. 'I can go wherever I like now because I can change my size whenever I want. But I'll stay the same size for the time being because I can see a very odd house down there by the bend in the path. I must go and see who lives there.'

Alice was very disappointed when she went into the house and found herself in a dark, smoky kitchen, where the noise was so loud that she had to block her ears. When her eyes had grown used to the dark and had stopped watering, Alice saw a very strange scene before her. An enormous woman was sitting on a tiny stool in the middle of the room, violently shaking a bawling baby whose cries rent the air. A magnificent Cheshire cat was placidly watching the scene, with a smile that stretched right from one ear to the other.

'Good day, Madam,' Alice managed to say, between two of the baby's wails.

'Curtsey when you speak to me,' snapped the bad-tempered woman. 'I am a Royal Duchess and a lady-in-waiting to her Majesty the Queen.'

'I do beg your pardon,' said Alice, blushing. 'You must be the white rabbit's partner . . . He speaks most highly of you,' she added quickly, hoping to soften the angry duchess's mood.

'And where exactly is that white-furred snail? bellowed the unpleasant lady. 'We shall be late for the royal game of croquet and the queen will have his head cut off if he upsets her guests.'

182

'He won't be long,' said Alice quickly, horrified by the terrible threat. She cleared her throat. 'Excuse me, your Grace,' she asked, 'why does the Cheshire cat smile all the time?'

'What,' said the duchess in astonishment, 'don't you know that Cheshire cats always have that stupid smile on their faces all day long?'

'It's the first time I've come across it, your Grace,' Alice confessed with embarrassment.

'Well, you're very stupid,' raged the duchess, 'and not fit for anything but rocking the baby. Here, take this child. I'm going to look for my ridiculous partner!' And she shoved the baby into the flabbergasted Alice's arms and flounced away with a great deal of fuss and noise.

The cat helped Alice out of her difficulty by suggesting that she put the sleepy child in its cradle and follow him into the garden. He immediately leapt on to his favourite branch and, to Alice's amazement, his body vanished in a puff of stardust, leaving only his face with its wide grin.

'You are very handsome,' Alice said to him, trying to make conversation. 'Please will you tell me where you come from?'

'I am the last in line of a famous breed of cats and I have been sent to this strange kingdom to observe the customs of the Royal Family,' the cat replied graciously.

'I am very shocked by the Duchess's bad manners,' Alice admitted, 'but I would very much like to meet the Queen. Do you think I could join in her Majesty's game of croquet? And do you know where it is going to take place?'

'This path will lead you straight to the croquet lawn,' said the Cheshire Cat. 'I am sure the Queen will be delighted to have another player in her team, but be careful. She has an even worse temper than the Duchess. I might come and keep an eye on you, just in case anything happens. My best friend is a Gryphon and he might be able to help you if you need him. You can trust in him, have no fear.'

Alice thanked the kind Cheshire cat and went the way he had said, nibbling the magic mushroom so that she would grow back to her right size. Soon she saw a vast lawn in front of her. A very strange troop of Royal guards were marching across it. They had very flat bodies and tapering arms and legs which stuck out of each corner of their bodies.

'They are playing cards,' said Alice to herself. The Court was marching across the lawn, led by the Queen. 'The Queen of Hearts,' thought Alice, 'and the King and Knave of Hearts.' Everyone was brandishing pink flamingoes which they were going to use as mallets.

Alice could not help laughing at the stupefied look on the faces of the poor flamingoes. As for the croquet balls, they were the funniest things she had ever seen and quite impossible to control, much to the annoyance of the players. They were a family of little hedgehogs, and

they rolled through the hoops that the Royal guards made by bending over and putting their hands on the ground.

'What is your name, little girl?' boomed the Queen. 'Alice, your Majesty,' said Alice with a curtsey.

'Guards, give the child a game,' commanded the Queen. Alice did her best to control her strange mallet, despite the baleful looks it gave her whenever she missed a point, and she wasted a lot of time looking for her ball, who kept wandering off to quarrel with his brothers. It was chaos on the croquet lawn and everyone kept arguing. Alice got tired of it and called to the Cheshire cat to take her away from the game. He quickly sent the Gryphon to fetch her, and the strange beast carried Alice away on his back to the banks of an artificial lake,

where a little turtle from the Tropics was languishing.

'How nice of you to pay me a visit,' sighed the turtle. 'And what a pretty little girl! Tell me, my dear, would you like to hear all about my life in the Tropics?' Alice did not have the chance to answer because the turtle started to talk about his homeland straight away.

'I used to play hide and seek amongst the coral reefs with my sisters,' he said. 'The sea was so warm and so easy to swim in that we did not even have to paddle our feet.'

'Tell us about the parties and balls that you used to have,' said the Gryphon.

'Well,' said the little turtle, as if dreaming out loud, 'we often used to have big parties. Our friends, the dolphins, would organise a water

ballet, then there would be seahorse races . . . How sorry I am now that I was naughty and left my sisters! Now I spend my dreary days in this ridiculous little pool of stagnant water.'

The poor turtle began to cry. Alice felt very sorry for him and tried to console him. She and the Gryphon said goodbye to the sad turtle and promised to visit him again soon, then they flew away to have tea with the Gryphon's friend, the hatter.

The Gryphon took Alice to a clearing where a long table was laid with all sorts of dishes and cakes. Alice was very surprised to see how many cups and saucers there were, considering the small number of guests.

The hatter, a jolly little man, asked her to sit down in an armchair.

'Sit down, my dear,' he said. 'We are going to try some of the excellent tea the March hare is bringing us.'

'It really is delicious,' sighed a tired little voice. To her astonishment Alice saw a little dormouse slumped at the table with its eyes half closed.

'Excuse my curiosity,' said Alice, 'but why have you got so much china for so few guests?'

'Something very sad happened to us,' said the hatter sorrowfully. 'Every evening at five o'clock the three of us – the March hare, the dormouse and myself – had to wind up every clock in the kingdom, to make sure that they all chimed at the same time for the Royal tea. Alas, one evening we spent so long listening to the tales of our friend, the dormouse, that we forgot all about the clocks. The Queen accused us of killing time and condemned us to an eternal teatime where time has stopped.'

'It's a very cruel punishment,' sighed the dormouse. 'I don't have time to go to sleep any more and the sight of those never-ending cakes makes me feel sick.'

'As for the china,' said the hatter, 'we never have the time to wash

it up. But listen, there goes the Court's trumpet. We must hurry. Come along,' he said to Alice, 'or the Queen will be angry.'

The four of them started to run, dragging the dormouse along with them, still yawning pitifully. The March hare and the hatter had great difficulty balancing the cups of tea that they were condemned to drink for ever.

The courtroom was full. The jury's bench was occupied by several animals, who were all busy writing their names down on slates. Alice immediately noticed a dear little green lizard who was concentrating very hard on his writing, with his tongue out. The unfortunate Knave of Hearts was chained to the prosecutor's bench, looking very downhearted. The white rabbit was dressed up as a Royal herald and looked very important. The King and Queen were sitting high up on their thrones and they were both looking very severe.

'The Knave of Hearts stands accused of having secretly stolen the tarts which were baked for her Majesty's tea,' called the white rabbit. 'Calling the first witness. Will the hatter please stand.'

'Here I am, your Honour, I mean your Majesty,' stammered the hatter, who was still clutching his sandwich and his cup of tea. 'I'm afraid I haven't finished my tea yet,' he said, biting his saucer in his confusion. The jury laughed and the Queen went red with anger.

'Take him away, off with his head, off with his hat!' she roared, showing what seemed to Alice a remarkable lack of logic.

'Calling the second witness', trumpeted the white rabbit. 'Will the dormouse please stand! Where *is* the dormouse?' he asked anxiously, when there was no sound of movement.

A discreet snoring soon told him where. The second witness was fast asleep a mere two steps away from the judge's bench.

'Take him away! Shave off his whiskers, off with his head and throw him into prison!' shrieked the Queen at the top of her voice, turning puce with rage.

Alice was still trying to understand the Queen's contradictory commands when to her great astonishment she heard her name called.

It could not have been a worse time because she had just started to grow very fast again. So when she stood up, she knocked over the entire jury and caused a commotion.

'What is going on?' stammered the frightened king. 'Would the witness kindly put the jury back in their places? In their *proper* places,' he added severely. Alice realised that in her confusion she had put the little lizard back upside down and he couldn't turn back the right way up on his own. She gently gave the jury back their slates and helped to put the benches back. Then she took her place in the witness box. Her head was already touching the ceiling and she had plenty of opportunity to admire the jewels in the Royal crowns.

'Witness Alice,' said the King, 'Do you like cakes?'

'Yes, of course I do,' said the unsuspecting Alice with a smile.

'Then you are guilty!' brayed the Queen triumphantly. 'It was you who stole my favourite tarts! Besides, you are very bad at croquet! Off with her head at once!'

'But I haven't taken anything. I haven't stolen anything!' protested the unfortunate Alice, panic-stricken and about to burst into tears. 'I want to see a lawyer,' she added in despair.

Just then she realised that she was her normal size once more and the situation suddenly seemed very funny because she was enormous compared with everyone else and they all looked as tiny as insects.

'Why you're nothing but a pack of cards!' cried Alice. 'Goodbye to you!' and she turned and ran away, just as the cards were throwing themselves at her.

When she woke up on the riverbank, Alice spent a long time thinking about her marvellous dream of Wonderland.

FABLES
OF
LA FONTAINE

English Translation by Angela Wilkes

The Tortoise and the Hare

There is no point in rushing: the important thing is to be steady and punctual. The story of the tortoise and the hare proves this.

'If we have a race, I bet you I will win,' said the tortoise to the hare.

'You win? Are you mad?' retorted the hare

rashly. 'I think you have been in the sun too long, my friend.'

'Mad or not,' said the tortoise, 'I'm keeping to my bet.'

So the two of them agreed on the conditions of the race and what the prize was going to be.

The hare could have completed the course in just four leaps – I mean the sort of leaps he took when he was being chased by dogs and was trying to lose them. 'I have all the time in the world,' he said to himself. 'I can have something to eat, rest and sniff which way the wind is blowing.' So he let the tortoise set off at a gentlemanly pace.

The tortoise went as fast as he could, which was a slow but steady pace. The hare, however, thought nothing of the race. He was confident that he would win easily and thought he would just look foolish if he set off straight away. He nibbled some grass, had a little rest and played around. All of a sudden he saw that the tortoise had almost finished the race. He shot off like an arrow, but his burst of speed was to no avail and the tortoise won.

'Ha ha!' said the tortoise. 'I was right. What use is speed? I won. Just think what would have happened if you had had to carry your house on your back, like me!'

The Iron Pot and the Earthenware Pot

The iron pot suggested to the earthenware pot that they go for a walk. The earthenware pot said that he would rather stay safely by the fire because it would only take the slightest knock to shatter him. 'It's all right for you,' he said. 'You are much tougher than me. There's nothing to stop you from going.'

'I will look after you,' said the iron pot. 'If anything hard

comes along and looks as if it is going to bump into you, I will step in the way and protect you from the blow.'

The earthenware pot was reassured by this, so the two pots set off close together. They clippity-clopped along on their three feet as best they could, knocking into each other every time they came to a bump. The earthenware pot suffered as a result. Before they had even gone a hundred steps he was smashed into tiny pieces by his companion, without even having a chance to complain.

Only mix with your equals, or you might meet the same fate as the earthenware pot!

The Milkmaid
and the Jug of Milk

Polly boasted that she could carry a jug of milk on her head all the way to town without spilling it. She strode along with the jug of milk balanced on a cushion on her head. She was lightly dressed in a short skirt and flat shoes, which she had put on specially, so that she could walk more easily.

As she went along, she was already working out in her head how much money she would get for the milk and what she would do with it. She would buy a hundred eggs and get three lots of chicks from them. Everything would go as planned, thanks to her skill and care. 'After all,' she said to herself, 'It will be easy for me to raise chickens round my house. With any luck the fox will leave enough of them for me to buy a pig with the money I get. It won't take much bran to fatten him up and when he's a reasonable size I'll sell him for more than I paid for him. And there's no reason why I shouldn't get a cow and a calf to put in the cowshed, seeing how much money I'll have.

Before I know it, there'll be a whole herd of cows.'

Polly was so carried away by her daydreaming that she tripped and the jug of milk went tumbling: farewell calf, cow, pig and poultry. The mistress of all this wealth cast a sorrowful eye on the fortune she had just spilt and went to make her excuses to her husband, in the hope that he wouldn't give her a hiding. The story soon became a joke locally, and people called Polly 'Milk jug'.

Doesn't everyone build castles in Spain, like Polly? Every Tom, Dick and Harry, no matter how sensible they normally are? Everyone daydreams, there is nothing nicer. We can be carried away by some charming illusion and we think the world is our oyster and that fame and fortune are there for the taking. When I am on my own, I imagine that I can stand up to any man. I can overthrow powerful rulers, be made King and be adored by all my subjects, and have honours heaped upon me. Then some little thing brings me back down to Earth again and I am good old John again, just the same as before.

The Fox
and the Stork

One day the fox went to some expense and asked his friend the stork to dinner. The meal was small and simple and the gallant fox only served a clear broth, for he lived very humbly. He served the broth in a dish, so the stork, with her long beak, couldn't eat any of it at all and the crafty fox lapped it all up in a few minutes.

Some time later, in revenge for this trick, the stork invited the fox to dinner. 'I'll come with pleasure,' said the fox. 'I don't stand on ceremony with my friends.'

He ran to the stork's house at the appointed time, complimented his hostess and remarked that the dinner looked as if it was cooked to

a turn. He was very hungry, for foxes always are. He smacked his lips at the smell of the meat cooking. It was cut up into tiny pieces and looked delicious. But to make things difficult for the fox, the stork served the meal in a vase with a long, thin neck and a very narrow opening. The stork could easily get her beak into it, but the fox's nose was far too broad. He went back home with his tail between his legs and his ears flat, looking as shamefaced as if he had been caught by a hen.

Beware, tricksters, this story is for you.

You only get as good as you give!

The Frog who wanted to be as big as a Bull

A frog saw a bull and thought what a fine size he was. The frog himself was hardly any bigger than an egg. He was very envious of the bull, so he huffed and puffed and tried to make himself the same size as the bull.

'Look at me,' he said to his sister. 'Is that enough? Am I big enough yet?'

'No,' said his sister.

'Am I there yet?'

'Far from it.'

Then the silly creature puffed himself up so much that he burst.

The world is full of people as stupid as the frog. They want to be grander than they really are. Every nobody wants to be a great lord and every minor prince wants to be a great king.

The Fox
and the Crow

The crow was sitting up in a tree, holding a piece of cheese in his beak. The fox came along and the smell of the cheese made him feel hungry.

'Good day to you, Mr. Crow,' he said. 'How handsome you are. If your singing matches up to your looks, you must truly be the king of the woods.'

The crow's chest swelled with pride at these words. He opened his beak to show off his fine voice and dropped the piece of cheese. The fox grabbed it.

'My good Mr. Crow,' he said, 'it's about time you learnt that flattery is costly to those who are silly enough to pay any attention to it. Surely that lesson is worth a piece of cheese.'

The crow was very embarrassed and ashamed, and swore that no-one would make a fool of him again.

The Elephant and the Rat

One day a very small rat saw a very big elephant and sneered at how slowly the noble beast moved. On his back the elephant was carrying a famous sultan, the sultan's dog, cat, monkey, parrot, old mother and all his wordly goods, because they were going on a pilgrimage. The rat was astonished that people were impressed by the mighty animal.

'He isn't more important than me just because he's bigger!' he said. 'What do all you people see in him? Are you impressed by that huge body which frightens children? Small as we rats are, we don't think we are any less important than the elephants.' He would have carried on, but just then a cat came along and showed him in less than a second that a rat is not the same as an elephant.

The Fisherman and the Little Fish

A little fish will grow into a big fish as long as he lives long enough! But it would be foolish to let him go in the meantime, for who knows if you would ever catch him again?

One day a very small carp was caught by a fisherman standing on the riverbank. 'Every little thing counts,' said the fisherman when he saw what he had caught. 'I'll put it in my gamebag and I might catch something bigger next time.'

'What use am I to you?' asked the poor little carp. 'I won't even provide you with half a mouthful. Let me go. I'll grow into a big carp and you will catch me again later. Someone will pay you a good price for me and it will save you the trouble of having to catch another hundred small fish like me to make a meal. It wouldn't be worth the trouble.'

'Well, that's your opinion,' said the fisherman. 'Preach as you may, my dear fish, you are going into the frying pan. It's all very well talking, but you are going to be cooked this evening. It's better to have a small fish like you now than take a chance of catching a bigger one later on. I have you here and now, but I can't be sure that I will have anything in the future!'

The Hen Who Laid Golden Eggs

People who are too greedy and want to have everything can lose what they already have, as this story shows.

There was once a man who had a hen which laid a golden egg every day. The man thought she must have some treasure inside her, so he killed her and opened her up, to find she was exactly the same as all the hens who laid ordinary eggs. He had in fact destroyed his finest treasure.

Let this be a lesson to greedy people. Just think how many people there are who have lost everything they had within a day, simply because they were too eager to get rich.

The Town Mouse and

One day the town mouse cordially invited the country mouse to come and have dinner with him. The meal was laid out on the finest Turkish carpet and the food was sumptuous. The two friends had everything they needed for a really magnificent feast. But as they were eating, someone disturbed their little party. They heard a sound at the door of the room and the town mouse fled, with the country mouse hot on his heels.

the Country Mouse

When the noise stopped, the town mouse said to his friend,

'Let's go back and finish our dinner.'

'No, I've had enough,' said his rustic friend. 'You can come and have dinner with me tomorrow. I don't pride myself on providing a feast fit for a king, like you, but at least I can eat my dinner in peace, without being disturbed. What use is luxury if you are too scared to enjoy it?'

217

The Cat, the Weasel and the little Rabbit

One fine morning the weasel moved into the young rabbit's home.

It was a trick. Nothing could have been easier, as the rabbit was out. The weasel moved all her things in when he had gone to greet the dawn, amongst the dewy thyme. When the rabbit had grazed and scampered about and done everything he had to do, he went back to his underground home and saw the weasel at the window.

'My goodness, who is that? said the now homeless rabbit. 'Come out without making a fuss, Mrs. Weasel, or I will tell the local rats about it.'

The weasel replied that the place belonged to the first person to get there. 'What a ridiculous place to fight over,' thought the rabbit.

'Even I have to crawl to get into it.'

'Even if this were a kingdom,' said the weasel, 'I would like to know if there is any law saying that this home should belong to you rather than to anyone else.'

'Custom,' said the rabbit. 'That is the law which has made me lord and master of this burrow and which has passed it down from father to son, from Peter to Simon and then to me. Is the rule of first come, first served really any better?'

'Let's ask the cat,' said the weasel.

The cat lived like a devout hermit and behaved as if butter wouldn't melt in his mouth. He was saintly looking cat, big, fat and furry, and an expert arbitrator in cases like this. The rabbit agreed

that the cat should judge the case and the two of them went off to consult his furry Majesty.

The cat said to them,

'Come closer, my children. I am old and hard of hearing.'

Trustingly they both went nearer. The minute the two contestants were within paw's reach, the saintly cat grabbed the pair of them and settled the argument by eating them both.

This is often what happens when petty rulers take their grievances to a king.

The Ant and the Grasshopper

The grasshopper sang all summer long, but when the cold winter came, she found that she hadn't got a single morsel to eat, not even as much as a fly or a worm. She went to her neighbour, the ant, saying she was starving, and begged her to lend her enough grain to last until the summer.

'I promise I will repay you everything with interest before August,' she said.

The ant did not like lending anything. 'What were you doing when the weather was good?' she asked the grasshopper.

'I sang all day and all night long,' replied the grasshopper.

'You sang? Well, that's nice,' said the ant. 'Now you can dance for a change.'

The Wolf and the Lamb

The stronger person is always right, as you are about to find out.

One day a lamb was drinking from a clear stream, when a hungry wolf came along, looking for trouble.

'What a cheek you have, dirtying my drinking water,' said the wolf angrily. 'You shall be punished for this.'

'Please don't be angry, Sir,' said the lamb. 'I am drinking the water at least twenty steps downstream from you, so I can't possibly be dirtying your drinking water.'

'You are dirtying it,' said the cruel wolf, 'and I know that you insulted me last year.'

'How could I have insulted you?' said the lamb, 'I wasn't even born then. I am still drinking my mother's milk now.'

'If it wasn't you, it must have been your brother,' said the wolf.

'I haven't got a brother,' replied the lamb.

'Then it was another one of your family,' said the wolf. 'None of you lot have a kind word to say about me, nor have your shepherds or their dogs. I know, and you deserve to be punished.'

And with that, the wolf carried the lamb away into the forest and ate him without any further ado.

The Jay who dressed up in Peacock's feathers

A peacock was moulting and a jay took his feathers and dressed up in them. Then he strutted around proudly amongst the other peacocks, thinking how handsome he looked.

Somebody recognised him and everyone scoffed and jeered at him and made fun of him. The peacocks plucked him, so that he looked very odd, and even when he went back to take refuge amongst his fellow jays, he was shooed away.

There are quite a few jays like him who like to dress up in other people's cast-offs. Some people call them copy-cats. I don't say anything. I don't want to cause any trouble. After all, it's none of my business.

The Two Mules

Two mules were walking along together. One of them was laden with oats and the other one was carrying the tax money. The tax mule was very proud to be carrying such an important load and wouldn't have given it up for anything. He trotted along jauntily, ringing his little bell. Suddenly a band of robbers appeared and stopped the tax mule. They grabbed his reins and covered him with blows. As he was defending himself he whimpered,

'Is this what I was promised? The mule behind me escapes scot free and I have to die because of what I am carrying.'

'It's not always a good thing to have such an important job, my friend,' his companion said to him. 'If you had just worked for a miller, like me, you would not have have had to suffer.'

The Oak Tree and the Reed

One day the oak tree said to the reed,

'You must be very annoyed with Nature. A wren is too heavy for you and the slightest breeze which ruffles the water makes you bend your head, whereas I am like a mountain and can stand up to both the sun and the storms. Every wind seems like the North Wind to you and just a balmy breeze to me. You wouldn't have to suffer so much if you were born in the shade of my lofty branches, but you are usually born on damp, windswept banks. I think that Nature has been very unkind to you.'

'It's good of you to be so concerned,' replied the reed, 'but do not worry. I have less to fear from the winds than you. I bend and do not break. Up until now you have stood up to their frightful blowing without bending your back, but just you wait and see what happens.'

Just as he said this, the most terrible North Wind came blowing along. The tree stood up to it and the reed bent. The wind blew even harder, so hard that it uprooted the tree, whose head was in the heavens and whose feet were touching the kingdom of the dead.

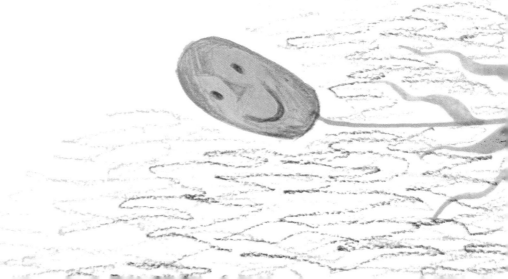

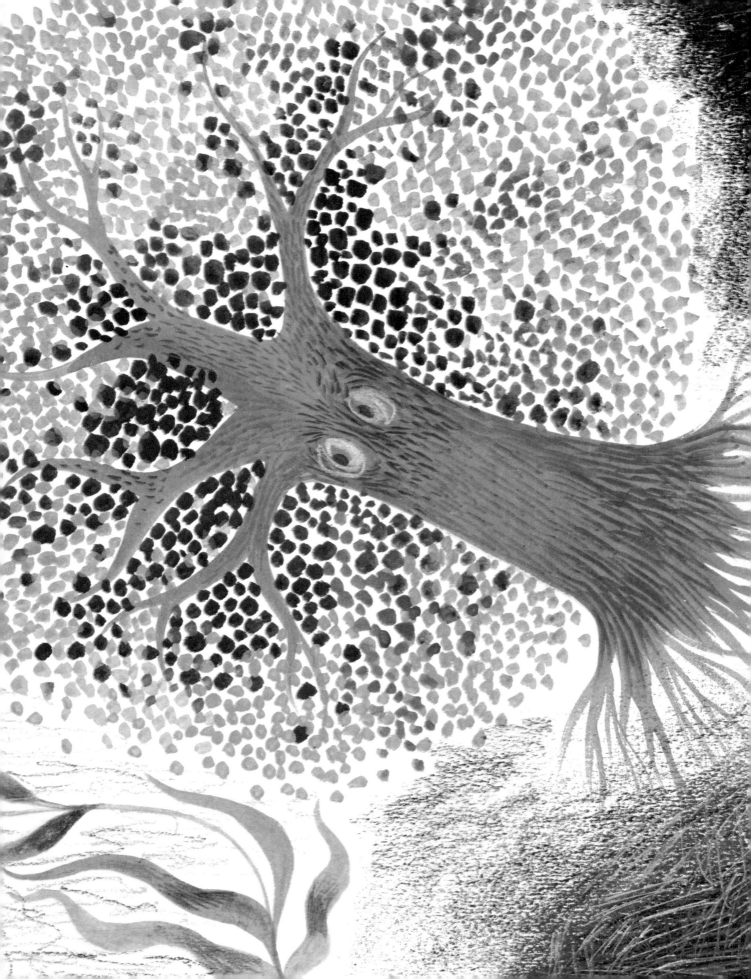

The Weasel who went into the Storehouse

The long, slender weasel managed to get into a storehouse through a very small hole. There she lived like a queen, eating and gnawing her way through everything she could find. She ended up plump and well-rounded with bulging cheeks. At the end of the week, when she had eaten her fill, she heard a noise and wanted to leave through the hole, but she could not get through it and thought she must have made a mistake. She went all round the storehouse a few times. 'That must be the right hole,' she thought. 'How strange. I managed to get through it five or six days ago.'

A rat, who had seen what was happening, said,

'You had a bit less of a belly then. You were thin when you came in; you will have to be thin to go out.'

This is the sort of thing one often says to others, but just remember that their business is none of yours.

The Dove and the Ant

A dove was drinking from a clear stream one day when an ant fell into the water. It tried to reach the bank, but couldn't, so the dove went to its rescue at once. She held a leaf into the water and the ant used it to climb back on to land, safe and sound.

Just then a local lad was passing by with a crossbow in his hands. The moment he saw the dove, he imagined her in his stewpot and smacked his lips. He was just about to shoot her when the ant nipped him on the heel. The villain turned his head and the dove heard him and flew away, taking his supper with her. One good turn deserves another.

The Cockerel and the Pearl

One day a cockerel came across a pearl as he was scratching about on the ground, and he gave it to the first jeweller he met. 'I think it's a good pearl,' he said, 'but even the smallest grain of millet would be of more use to me.'

A man who couldn't read inherited a manuscript, which he took to his neighbour, a bookseller. 'I think it's a good book,' he said, 'but even a few pennies would be of more use to me.'